THE OUTLA

C000244166

JENNIFER ASH has taken the medieval part of "*Romancing Robin Hood*", written by her alter ego Jenny Kane, and turned it into the standalone novel "*The Outlaw's Ransom*". But whereas Jenny Kane writes cosy Sunday afternoon contemporary fiction with a hint of romance, and a feel good factor, Jennifer Ash writes medieval mysteries with an edge of uncertainty - albeit with a hint of romance in the background.

This book is the first one of "*The Folville Chronicles*" and is followed by the medieval sequel "*The Winter Outlaw*" (Book 2, out in April 2018). Book 3 in this series, "*Edward's Outlaw*", will be released at the end of 2018/early 2019.

Happy reading,

Ash xx

JENNIFER ASH

THE

OUTLAW'S RANSOM

COPYRIGHT

Littwitz Press
Dahl House, Brookside Crescent
Exeter EX4 8NE

First published in Great Britain by Accent Press in 2016

www.littwitzpress.com

A CIP catalogue record for this book is available
from the British Library.

ISBN: 978-1-9998552-6-0

Acknowledgements

With thanks to Professor Norman Housely of the
University of Leicester for putting up with me as an eager
PhD student so many years ago.

To Barnaby Eaton-Jones for allowing me
to thank so many of the influences in my life in person.

To Steve – who has had to share me with
Robin Hood for a very long time. X

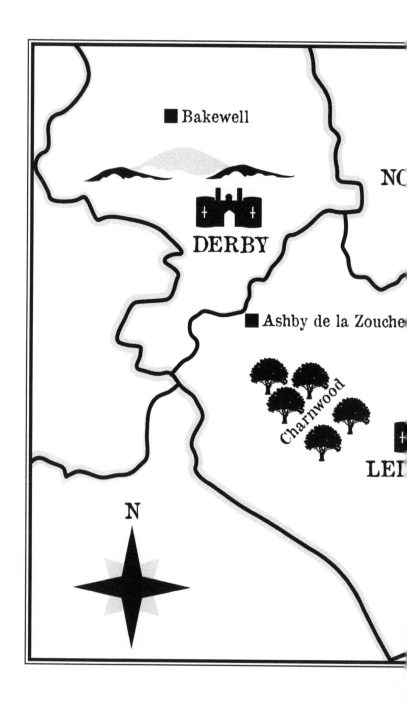

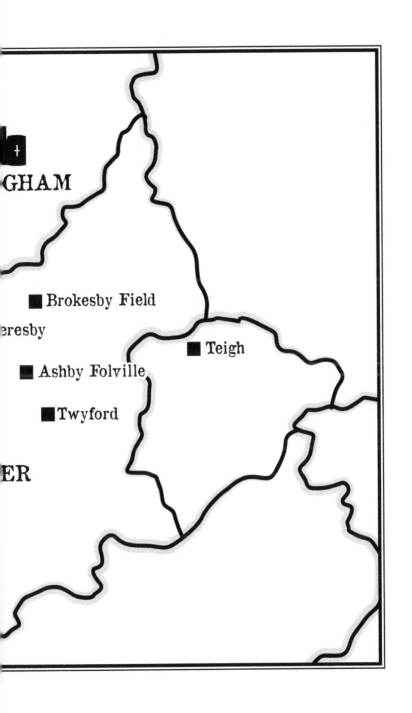

~ *Chapter One* ~

Mathilda thought she was used to the dark, but the night-time gloom of the small room she shared with her brothers at home was nothing like this. The sheer density of this darkness enveloped her, physically gliding over her clammy skin. It made her breathless, as if it was trying to squeeze the life from her.

As moisture oozed between her naked toes, she presumed that the suspiciously soft surface she crouched on was moss, which had grown to form a damp cushion on the stone floor. It was a theory backed up by the smell of mould and general filthiness which hung in the air.

Trying not to think about how long she was going to be left in this windowless cell, Mathilda stretched her arms out to either side and bravely felt for the extent of the walls, hoping she wasn't about to touch something other than cold stone. The child's voice that lingered at the back of her mind, even though she was a woman of nineteen, was telling her – screaming at her – that there might be bodies in here, secured in rusted irons, abandoned and rotting. She battled the voice down. Thinking like that would do her no good at all. Her father had always congratulated his only daughter on her level-headedness, and now it was being so thoroughly put to the test, she was determined not to let him down.

Stretching her fingers into the blackness, Mathilda placed the tips of her fingers against the wall behind her. It was wet. Trickles of water had found a way in from somewhere, giving the walls the same slimy covering as the floor.

Continuing to trace the outline of the rough stone wall, Mathilda kept her feet exactly where they were. In seconds her fingertips came to a corner and by twisting at the waist, she quickly managed to plot her prison from one side of the heavy wooden door to the other. The dungeon could be no more than five feet square, although it must be about six feet tall. Her own five-foot frame had stumbled down a step when she'd been pushed into the cell, and her head was at least a foot clear of the ceiling. The bleak eerie silence was eating away at Mathilda's determination to be brave, and the cold brought her suppressed fear to the fore. Suddenly the shivering she had stoically ignored overtook her, and there was nothing she could do but let it invade her.

Wrapping her thin arms around her chest, Mathilda pulled up her hood, hugged her grey woollen surcoat tighter about her shoulders and sent an unspoken prayer of thanks to Our Lady for the fact that her legs were covered.

She'd been helping her two brothers, Matthew and Oswin, to catch fish in the deeper water beyond the second of Twyford's fords when the men had come. Mathilda had been wearing an old pair of Matthew's hose, rolled up past her knees, but no stockings or shoes. She thought longingly of her warm footwear, discarded earlier with such merry abandon. She'd thrown haphazardly beneath a tree in her eagerness to join the boys in their work. It was one of the only jobs their father gave them that could have been considered fun.

Mathilda closed her eyes, angry as the tears she'd forbidden herself to shed defied her and fell anyway. With them came weariness. It consumed her, forcing her to sink lower onto the rotten floor. Water dripped into her lank red hair. The tussle of her capture had loosened Mathilda's neatly woven plait, and now it hung awkwardly, half in and half out of its bindings, like a badly strapped sheaf of straw.

She tried not to start blaming her father, but it was difficult not to. Why hadn't he told her he'd borrowed money from the Folvilles? It was an insane thing to do. Only the most desperate …

Mathilda stopped her thoughts in their tracks. They were disloyal and pointless.

They'd been relatively well-off when Mathilda was younger. They'd owned four horses, chickens, a cow and a goat, three furlongs for planting vegetables and a small amount of wheat. There was also the pottery shed and kiln where her father made his tableware and cooking pots, and a small orchard which backed onto the two-roomed house. Slowly, over the past few years, it had almost all been sold off. Only the workhouse, orchard, one horse and cart, and a single furlong remained.

Now she had nothing to do but think, Mathilda realised that her father had been that desperate. He'd been a tall man once, but since his forty-fifth year he'd dwindled, his beard dappled with more grey by the day. It was as if he'd become disillusioned; fed up with the routine of daily existence without her mother. Until now, Mathilda had been so busy making the best of things, she hadn't had time to see their situation for what it was.

Since her mother had died four years ago, the cooler weather and the disastrous crop failure a few harvests back, combined with the decline in the demand for locally made pottery had taken their toll. Ceramic tableware from the south, Wales and even France flooded the market, and her father hadn't been able to compete. Each time he travelled the ten miles to the weekly market at Leicester to sell his pots, he came home more dejected than the trip before and with more and more unsold stock.

Last time her father had travelled into Leicester he'd returned home early, a desolate figure, with a cartload of shattered pottery shards. A thief had struck in the market place and in their unthinking eagerness to apprehend the villain, the bailiff's men had run roughshod through the stalls, toppling her father's table as they went, leaving him with broken stock and an increasingly broken faith.

'Our Lady,' Mathilda muttered in the gloom, her voiced hushed in fear, 'please deliver me from this place.' Then, guilty at having asked for something so boldly from someone she'd begun to neglect of late, Mathilda added, 'I'm sorry, Our Lady, forgive me. I'm frightened, that's all. Perhaps, though, you could take care of my brothers and my father.'

Mathilda didn't even know if any of her kin were still alive. The Folvilles' reputation made it more than possible that they'd all been killed.

The men had taken her so easily; lifting her bodily from the water as if she was as light as air. Bundled into a covered wagon, Mathilda had been transported to the manor at Ashby Folville in the company of a large man who stank of fish. He'd tied her hands behind her back and sat over her, shoving a filthy rag between her lips to fend off the protests that failed to escape from her mouth.

The journey, although bumpy and bruising, couldn't have been further than two miles. On arrival Mathilda had been untied and un-gagged and, having been thoroughly stared at from top to bottom by her impertinent guardian, who seemed to have the ability to see through her clothes to the flesh beneath, was wordlessly bundled below stairs to her current lonely location. Her stomach growled, complaining pointlessly at its emptiness. Mathilda was cross with herself. How could she even consider food when her family was in danger?

'Just as well I don't want to eat,' she told herself sternly, 'as I probably won't ever see food again.' Then she collapsed to the cold damp ground, the terror and shock of the morning abruptly washing over her in a wave of misery.

Mathilda had no idea how long she'd been in the cell when a large hand gripped her shoulder and shook her awake. Fear crept back over her like a heavy blanket as the light from the adjoining room illuminated the mocking face of her gaoler.

'You're wanted, girl.' Dragging her by the arm, he took no notice of the fact he was bumping her legs against the stone steps as he removed her from the prison.

'Where are you talking me?' Mathilda's voice wavered as she tried not to trip over her own feet.

'You'll see.' Increasing the squeeze of her upper arm, he propelled Mathilda along a corridor, before pushing her before him into a large open hall, shouting ahead, 'You want me to tie her up?'

Mathilda didn't hear anyone answer. The hall was foggy from a poorly set fire, and it took her a few moments to take in her surroundings as she was pushed towards a long table. The smoke stung her eyes, and she blinked against the light.

Her arms and feet hadn't been tied, but as a precaution against Mathilda's potential escape, the surly man stood uncomfortably close to her. Now her senses were slowly coming back under her control, Mathilda recognised him as the person who'd stolen here from her home. The unpleasant odour of ale, sweat and fish made his identity as her original kidnapper unmistakable.

As the fishy aroma assaulted Mathilda's nostrils once more, her thoughts flew to her brothers. Desperate for news of her family, she opened her mouth to speak, but another man raised his hand, warning for her to remain silent before the words had chance to form.

Mathilda stared at the shape of this new figure as he came properly into focus through the smoke. He was finely dressed in a peacock blue cloak, with a green and brown tunic and matching hose. Despite the fine braiding around his collar, she could tell this was not a man of high birth, nor was he the sheriff or bailiff. This probably made him one of the lesser nobility or a public servant.

Swallowing nervously, Mathilda lowered her gaze to the floor in a natural response at being before her betters – even if 'betters' was entirely the wrong description in this case. This man had to be a Folville. Mathilda began to shake with increased fear as a million possibilities of what might happen to her next flew around her brain. None of them were pleasant.

'You wish to ask questions,' His voice was husky but soft, without the harsh edge she'd been expecting, 'and yet you are keeping quiet. Perhaps, if I decide you deserve answers, then you will be given permission to speak. For now, I am asking the questions.'

Mathilda kept her eyes firmly on the dusty floor, concentrating on her cold bare feet.

'What is your name, child? What age are you?'

'Mathilda of Twyford. I'm nineteen, my Lord.'

'You appear younger.' He looked harder into her face for a second before carrying on. 'Tell me, Mathilda of Twyford, do you know the stories of Robyn Hode?'

Surprised by the question, Mathilda's head snapped up. She found herself meeting her captor's blue eyes. Was he one of the Folville brothers after all? His manner suggested not.

There was a grunt of derision from the large man Mathilda had come to think of as her jailer. Glaring over Mathilda's shoulder, straight at her escort, the richly dressed man spoke with a far cruder edge to his voice, 'I'm sure you must have parishioners to lead astray, brother. I can attend to this girl alone. You are dismissed.'

The religious Folville, the rector of Teigh? Surely the man who'd dragged her here couldn't be a man of the cloth? Mathilda had no time to speculate on this revelation however, for the man in blue was repeating his question. 'I asked if you knew the stories of Robyn Hode, child?'

'Why … yes, yes, I do, my Lord.'

Catching the gleam in his eyes, Mathilda remembered herself and hastily lowered her own eyes again, frightened of his reaction to her infraction.

He seemed more amused than cross at her boldness however. Mathilda was confused. She was convinced she could detect suppressed laughter in the man's voice as he continued, 'Well, Mathilda, can you tell me what Hode does?'

'He takes from rich people, my Lord and helps those he thinks deserve it.'

'That is almost correct. Although if you listen to the balladeers carefully next time they come to the fair, you'll notice that Hode takes from those who are cruel or greedy. They aren't necessarily rich.'

The man stood and came closer and stared at her stained clothing, filthy from the cell. His stare was doing nothing to calm the shake in Mathilda's shoulders. 'Do you enjoy the stories, Mathilda?'

'Yes, my Lord. My mother used to sing them, and I've heard them played at the fair, as you say.'

Satisfied with her answer, he confined, 'I particularly like the bit when Robyn Hode demands a tax from those passing through Barnsdale and how he punishes those who fail to discharge their debts.'

Bile rose in Mathilda's throat; so all this was about money. She wondered how much her father owed this man.

'Do you believe everyone should pay their debts?'

She tried to say 'Yes, my Lord,' but the words died in her throat as Mathilda visualised her father thrown into a cell like the one she'd so recently occupied, and her brothers, hurt or dead. The horrific pictures within her mind suddenly swam together in an incoherent blur. Her legs began to buckle …

~ *Chapter Two* ~

Mathilda awoke disorientated by her surroundings. Someone had placed her upon a rough straw stuffed pallet. A
makeshift tapestry divider was drawn at her side. As the
smoky atmosphere registered in her nostrils, she realised
she was still in the main hall of the Folvilles' establishment,
but had been moved to one of the servant's beds to recover
from her faint.

This act of consideration did not fit with what she'd
heard about the Folville family. Frantically trying to gather
her thoughts, Mathilda fixed her eyes on a mass of spider's
webs on the rafters above. Her father would have had plenty
to say if she'd allowed such a number of webs to amass in
their home.

Thinking of her father bought the thump of her head-
ache into sharper focus as she tried to remember what the
Folville had been saying to her before she'd disgraced herself. The question about Robyn Hode, hadn't been what she
would have expected either, nor was the semi-concealed
amusement of the man who'd asked it.

Mathilda had heard it said that Eustace de Folville would
rip your ears off with his bare hands if he so desired. There
was no way the man who liked Robyn Hode could be Eustace. On the other hand, she wasn't finding it at all difficult

to believe that her clergyman jailer had been a Folville. If that really had been Richard, rector of Teigh, his image certainly matched the mythology that rumour had spread about the family all over the shire, and himself in particular.

She'd heard stories about all of the brothers. Although they always seemed to slip through the fingers of the law whenever a crime occurred, Mathilda knew with certainly that the Folvilles had been responsible for the organisation of thefts, kidnaps, assaults and even the death of Baron Roger Belers three years earlier. Everyone knew.

The murder of a Baron of Exchequer had been the stuff of gossip ever since. Mathilda had been sixteen in that year, 1326, when the news that a gang of noblemen, led by the Folvilles, had joined forces to dispose of the old man. She remembered her father and brothers talking about Belers' death in hushed tones, more in awe and relief at the removal of such an unscrupulous man who'd acquired much of his land illegally, than in horror at the manner of his death. The careful talk behind hands had gone further: that two men Mathilda had never heard of before, Henry de Heredwyk and Roger la Zouche, had paid the Folvilles to remove the baron from the face of the earth.

No one had been properly tried for the crime, but at the same time, everyone knew who was responsible, and enough suspicion had arisen for the Folville family to have their lands at Reresby taken from them. It had been more of an official warning than a punishment. A gesture from those in charge. Nothing more.

Mathilda rubbed her forehead; it was hot and sticky despite the cool of the room, and she feared she might be feverish. Or perhaps it was sheer terror, as she contemplated the household's reputation. She closed her eyes against the industry of the spider above and fought against the urge to start shaking.

It had been shortly after Belers' death that Mathilda had asked her eldest brother, Matthew, about Eustace de Folville. He'd simply said, 'he commits evils' and refused to be drawn further, but that had been enough to make her determined to keep well away from the village and manor of Ashby Folville from then onwards.

Despite her natural curiosity, she hadn't enquired about the family after that; yet talk at the market and across the furlongs as her neighbours worked the land, meant that Mathilda knew the Folvilles had adopted crime as their chief way of making a living; although no one would have been foolish enough to accuse a Folville of criminal behaviour to his face. The brothers had made their presence felt beyond Ashby Folville, across the Hundred of East Goscote and indeed the whole county of Leicestershire.

Rising slowly, Mathilda's head still throbbed with a dull ache behind her eyes, but at least she no longer felt dizzy. The thought that she ought to try and escape crossed her mind, but realistically she knew that would be suicide, or worse, would endanger her family further. She felt as helpless as she felt useless. And how about right now? Should she sit where she was until someone came to tell her to move? Should she announce that she was awake?

Aware of voices beyond the tapestry curtain, Mathilda tensed as she heard the soft pad of approaching footsteps. Someone was moving across the hall towards where she lay. She gripped each side of the bed, her fingers digging into the wooden framework.

Her breath shot out between her lips in a rush of temporary relief as a lad pulled back the curtain.

'Good. My Lord Folville wishes you to return. Drink

and eat this.'

He had the air of being the kitchen boy. Evidently relieved to find Mathilda lucid, she suspected he'd probably been instructed to check on her every so often until she was fully conscious. Gladly taking the hunk of reasonably fresh bread and a small cup of ale, she ate and drank gratefully.

'Thank you.' She spoke in hushed tones to the boy, who silently watched while she chewed on a mouthful of bread in a manner which would have infuriated her father. He hated seeing anyone rush their food, in case there wasn't any more for a while. She could clearly hear her father's deep gravelly voice telling her off.

As the last traces of ale disappeared down her throat, Mathilda dabbed a few escaped breadcrumbs from her lap, bringing them to her lips before she whispered, 'What's your name? Can you tell me where I am?'

The lad, who she judged to be no more than twelve years old, was edgy and half glanced over his shoulder towards the fireplace as he replied. 'They call me Allward.' After a brief pause he added, 'this is Ashby Folville Hall, the home of his Lordship John Folville.'

As her fears were confirmed, Mathilda frowned. 'John? Not Eustace?'

Allward bowed, obviously uncomfortable. 'It is my Lord John's home, but he is here rarely. He prefers to reside in Leicester, or Huntingdon. The whole family live here. At times.'

'Was it my Lord John who bid me rest and eat?'

'No, miss, it wasn't.' The boy stood up. 'I'm instructed to take you back now.'

'Back to where?' An image of her cell suddenly loomed large, and an involuntary shiver rippled down Mathilda's spine.

The boy didn't answer, but merely walked away, beckoning her with an apologetic expression on his face which did nothing to calm Mathilda's fears.

She couldn't help but mutter with relief when she realised she was being taken, not back to the gaol, but to stand in the smoky hall, before the seated Folville in his blue cloak. No sooner had she arrived than he was talking to her as if no time had passed since her swoon.

'You are Mathilda of Twyford, daughter of Bertred of Twyford and sister to Matthew and Oswin?'

'Yes, my Lord,' Mathilda didn't know where to look, so she stared at her feet once again. She could feel the heat of his piercing eyes examining her closely.

'Do you remember what I asked you, Mathilda? Before you swooned.'

'Yes, my Lord,' Mathilda mumbled, before remembering her manners. 'Thank you for seeing me cared for, my Lord. I am sorry for the inconvenience I have caused.'

'You are welcome.'

She risked a glance at her noble companion's face, but it gave away nothing. Mathilda judged him to be in his twentieth year, maybe a little older. He was not pale or flabby enough to indicate a wholly indoor life, but nor was he tanned or muscled sufficiently to indicate an existence labouring in the fields or at a craft. She placed him as one of the younger brothers, with no specific role unless to fight as a knight for the king, or to enter the church. Not that she could imagine him in the latter role.

'So what were we saying, Mathilda?'

'I agreed that debtors should pay their debts, my Lord.'

'Good.' He stood and paced between her and the fire that now roared, without excess smoke but remained too fierce for safety, causing him to gesture to Allward to tame it. 'Sometimes debtors do not pay what they owe through sheer greed and so we, my brothers and I, have ways of sorting those affairs out.'

Mathilda's body tingled. A chill ran through her as this calm stranger, a stranger who'd so recently showed himself capable of kindness, now implied threats and violence.

'On other occasions, a debtor who is known to be otherwise honest is unable to pay what's owed on time. Or perhaps the debt is more complex than the mere owing of money. Chattels are used, sometimes crops or animals, or sometimes,' he paused again, his eyes assessing Mathilda shrewdly as he placed his hands on her shoulders, making her body tense beneath his firm touch, 'with the lending, or gift, of servants or younger members of the family.'

Letting go of her, the Folville crashed without dignity back onto his seat. 'These are turbulent times, Mathilda. King Edward the Second has been removed, and although his son sits upon the throne, it is common knowledge that Edward's queen, Isabella, and her favourite, the accursed Mortimer, really control this country. As the estates of that ribald fool Hugh Despenser, and the lands and policies of Thomas of Lancaster, are continually argued over, while our fair country's honour and that cursed land of Scotland is debated, who has an eye on the small towns of England? No one. No, we must look to ourselves, Mathilda; we must take care of our shire and protect it against injustice. Don't you agree?'

Mathilda nodded, more from duty than for any other reason. She hadn't understood a lot of what he'd said. Besides, her mind was filling with the realisation that her father not only saw her as a mere chattel, but had exchanged her, like a cow or a carved chest, as surety for his debt. The cold that hung about her, a quiet reminder of her small prison was feeling more intrusive by the second, and she had to fight to hide the shivers that were making her shoulders quake.

'I suspected, from what I'd heard from your father, that you were intelligent for a woman.'

The nobleman appeared pleased. Mathilda fought her confusion and, in order not to displease him, risked a reply. 'Thank you, my Lord. I see that, if you please, your family endeavours to protect the area; like Robyn Hode would if he were truly amongst us.' She added a hasty 'my Lord', in case she hadn't been supposed to speak.

If he'd been annoyed at her boldness, it didn't show. 'Indeed, girl, just like Hode would. A tragedy for the country that he is not amongst us.'

The Folville didn't say anything else, but satisfied himself with watching Mathilda as she stood, half bowed, before him. She wasn't shaking now. He'd noticed how hard she had fought within herself to still her external reactions to his news of her change in circumstance and had admired her self-control. It was almost as if she had an offended dignity about her rather than terror; an unusual reaction from a prisoner in the presence of a Folville.

He wondered if she'd been taught her letters. Most families didn't waste their time teaching their womenfolk such things, but Mathilda of Twyford was clearly sharp and capable. With her mother gone, she'd run the household, and he imagined she did that job well. He saw that his family's plan for this girl might work, but only if she kept that nerve. Otherwise… well, she wouldn't be the first to die during his family's quest to maintain their position.

Breaking the silence that had stretched out between them he said, 'I recall you have questions for me. I can see your head jarring with them.'

'If I may, my Lord?'

'You may, although I should caution you, I may not choose to offer a reply.'

Mathilda licked her lips and ran her clammy palms down her grubby belted surcoat, which largely hid her brother's leather hose, and flexed her numb bare toes.

'Please, my Lord, who are you?'

This produced a bark of laughter, 'You are well-mannered despite the indignity of being thrust, if only for a short while, into our cell. I am Robert de Folville, one of seven brothers of this manor.'

Mathilda curtsied, more out of natural impulse than any feelings of reverence towards this man, whom she knew for certain had been party to at least one murder. 'You are kin to my Lord Eustace, my Lord?'

'Yes, girl, I am.' He cocked his head to one side. 'That worries you?'

'He is a man I have been taught to fear, forgive my impudence, my Lord.'

He snorted. 'I would rather have honest impudence than bluff and lies. So, you have been instructed by your father to be wary of us?'

'Not only my father, sir.' Abruptly worried that her boldness might place her family in more danger, Mathilda clamped her mouth shut. Seeing, however, that the Folville wasn't cross, but had an expression of acceptance on his face, Mathilda braved a further question.

'Where is my father, my Lord, and Matthew and Oswin, my brothers?'

Robert de Folville paused and, after a moment's consideration, gestured for the servant boy to bring her a chair. Mathilda was glad to be allowed to sit down, but was puzzled at the equal status she was being afforded after her earlier abuse, as Folville sat next to her, leaning uncomfortably close to her slight, tense frame.

'Your father and your brother Matthew are at home in Twyford working on ways to pay back your debt. I do not know Oswin's whereabouts. I am, after all, only one of the younger brothers.'

Mathilda heard the bitterness in him and for the first time, she thought she understood something of this man. Robert de Folville would probably have made a good lord of the manor, but his lot was to be a minor son.

'You will have heard of the death of Belers almost three years hence?'

'Yes, my Lord.' Mathilda spoke softly as she thought back to the day she'd heard first about the murder on Brokesby Field. It may not have happened right on their doorstep, but the frisson of fear the crime had engendered had been felt even in Twyford; such was their closeness to the Folvilles' manor house; and the waves the crime had created were still leaving ripples these many months later.

He must have read her mind, for Robert slammed his hand against the table, making Mathilda jump. 'Damn it all girl! Roger Belers was a tyrant! An oppressive, rapacious man who had become a scourge on our county! We did what needed to be done. Hode would have done no less!'

Mathilda said nothing. It was clear he meant exactly what he said. His brothers probably did as well. They evidently believed they were providing a public service. They took their fee for such deeds as wages, just as the sheriff did when he arrested a felon for the King.

Folville leant towards Mathilda earnestly. 'Did your father ever sing you "The Outlaw's Song of Trailbaston", child?'

'I've heard of it, my Lord, but no, I don't know it as I

know the Robyn Hode tunes.'

'It contains much wisdom, Mathilda. I have no doubt that its great length influenced the author of the Hode stories.' Robert lounged back in his seat, his arms stretched behind his neck as he began to quote a verse to his captive.

'You who are indicted, I advise you, come to me,
To the green forest of Belregard, where there is no
annoyance
But only the wild animal and the beautiful shade;
For the common law is too uncertain.
What do you say, child?'

Mathilda swallowed again. The ale she'd drunk earlier had been stronger than she was used to. Her head ached, and her throat felt sticky, giving her a thirst worse than before. 'I believe there is wisdom within, my Lord. I have heard my elders say that the law is contradictory. If we truly have been abandoned by the law, perhaps you are correct to take matters into your own hands – within reason, my Lord.'

Mathilda flinched, expecting her host to strike out. She shouldn't have said that last bit. Why couldn't she ever keep her tongue in check? Her directness had always been frowned upon within her family, and now Mathilda was deeply regretting sharing her opinion honestly. She tensed, awaiting the call for a guard to come and throw her back into prison.

It did not come. Folville was peering at her quizzically, 'You are a curious creature, Mathilda of Twyford. You must realise you have been used to pay off your father's debts, but you ask nothing of your own future, only theirs. My reverend brother placed you in our cell, and you do not ask why, nor make complaint about your enclosure.'

Mathilda bit her tongue, not wanting to say the wrong thing, despite her desire for answers to the questions he'd posed.

'Your father told Eustace and the rector that you were headstrong and determined when they collected you. As a result, Richard decreed a spell in our holding cell to soften you to our will.' Robert snorted into his mug of ale. 'He obviously never bothered to take the time to speak to you himself before he acted. A fact about my holy brother that astounds me not one jot.'

Mathilda stared hard at the floor. The glimmer of a first smile since her kidnap was trying to form at the corner of her mouth, and she felt guilty for its presence.

She could feel Robert's blue eyes burning into the top of her bowed head. As he said, 'Your father vouched to Eustace that you have qualities more suited to a man than to the gentler sex. It seems you are happier in the river or fields than the house and only run the home as it is your duty as a woman.'

Giving no reply, Mathilda was glad Robert wasn't able to see her face, as she was unable to prevent the crimson blush of shame that came as she heard how her father had described her. Not only was she ashamed, she felt indignant. She'd worked ceaselessly to run the house, the remaining furlong and the orchard as successfully as her mother had done, even though it was a task she didn't enjoy and frequently resented.

'Well, Mathilda of Twyford, I will tell you what Eustace has demanded of your father.'

Mathilda sat up straighter and risked looking directly at her captor, clasping her hands in her lap as she listened.

'We have an adequate complement of servants here, Mathilda, so exchanging you for payment of a debt was a rather unusual thing for Eustace to do.'

Mathilda felt sick. A thousand unpleasant uses for her

swam through her mind.

'Eustace had considered selling you on. Servants and whores are always required,' Mathilda blanched at the casual manner in which Robert spoke of her potential disposal, 'but your father told him you were quick-witted and so my Lord Eustace had an idea of a more satisfying use for you and for us. Do you have letters?

'Some, my Lord, but only to read, not to write.'

'That is of no matter. Reading will be of help, and you'll be able to learn more without too much trouble if we need you to.'

A flicker of interest cut through Mathilda's troubled features. Perhaps they were less likely to sell her as a whore if they were enquiring about whether she'd been educated.

'You are to be our assistant and my companion. Do you think you could do that, Mathilda of Twyford?'

Mathilda's jaw dropped open, but no words came out. She gasped for air as she took in the narrowness of her escape from the shame of prostitution. Yet she couldn't help wonder if her soul would end up being in even worse peril if she was to stay within these walls for too long.

'Mathilda?'

'My Lord,' she gave another half-bow, images of her father and brothers forcing her to accept her immediate fate with a bravery she didn't feel, 'I will do my best to please you. But, if I may, sir, what sort of assistant?'

~ *Chapter Three* ~

Usually Mathilda bathed in the village ford, splashing about in an attempt to scrape off the flour, leaves, dirt and dust of daily life. Total immersion in a bath was a completely new experience for her.

When she'd been handed over to the austere female servant who'd been instructed to bathe her, Mathilda had been almost as frightened as when she'd been plucked from the cell to stand before the Folvilles.

Nothing that was happening to her made sense. Everything was changing so fast. Now she was being told to strip off her dirty, but familiar clothes and get into a wooden tub of water that steamed before the fire in a small room off the main hall.

Her fears, in this case at least, were unfounded. Plunged into the blissfully warm lavender-scented tub, the water unexpectedly soothed her undernourished body and eased her tense muscles. Mathilda sighed with the release of fear, even though she had no doubt it was only a temporary reprieve. While she immersed in that pool at least there was nothing she could do about anything except get clean. She found herself unexpectedly grateful for a period of forced inactivity, where she could neither receive instructions nor fruitlessly plot to run away.

I'm alive, she thought. And if, as Robert de Folville himself had told her, she'd been exchanged for a debt, then her family should also be alive and well enough to be able to work towards paying that debt off.

As the tight-lipped housekeeper undid the remaining ties of her hair and washed out its knotted tresses Mathilda resolved to believe that her new master was basically kind. It was less frightening that way. If the opportunity arose for her to ask about her family again, then she would do just that.

'Mathilda.'

Robert de Folville spoke sternly, and at once Mathilda could see why, unless you were very sure of yourself, it would be unwise to argue with his man.

It was as if he had two sides to him. A side that was never to be questioned, that was ruthless and determined and a kinder side, considerate of the individual and, most of all, the locality. It was how these two halves mixed and intertwined that intrigued Mathilda as she stood shyly before him in only her chemise.

The housekeeper who'd bathed her had produced fresh clothes for Mathilda, but despite all her experience and sharp temper, had been unable to persuade the ransomed girl to put them on; claiming that enough had happened to her, and she wanted to keep her own clothes on, no matter how worn they were. Eventually the older woman threatened to fetch his lordship to dress her himself, whether Mathilda was naked or not, and with grinning determination had fetched Robert.

Mathilda had only had time to wrap her arms around her modesty before Robert came striding in, annoyed impatience etched across his face. 'You will dress in these,' he pointed to the remainder of the pile of semi-new clothes. 'I can't waste my time with things like this, girl.'

Shaking her head firmly, Mathilda braced herself as she risked provoking his temper. The housekeeper was looking expectantly at Folville, and Mathilda suspected she was disappointed when Robert steadied his anger before speaking with deliberate clarity.

'Mathilda, it is important that you temper that natural directness of yours, not to mention your boldness. Those are valuable skills, but I need you to hide them beneath style and grace.' He pointed again to the garments laid out before them. 'These clothes will help you give the impression we require you to portray. Your own clothes will be cleaned and returned to you when the job is done.'

'You see my directness as a skill, my Lord?'

Robert almost smiled as he replied with exasperation, 'Boldness, intelligence, directness and an uncanny knack of knowing what's going on when you shouldn't may well get you out of here alive. But overconfidence will not be your friend.'

Mathilda's face flushed. 'I am no scandalmonger, my Lord.'

'I had not suggested such a thing. But as you prove to me once again, you are bold.' He turned to the housekeeper, treating the older woman to the edge of his simmering anger, 'Now, for the Lord's sake, Sarah, get some clothes on her. She looks like a whore.'

With that he stalked out of the room. Red with embarrassment, Mathilda allowed the disgruntled servant to help her into the fresh clothes. Over the chemise, she was pushed into a tightly sleeved dress of light brown, and on top of that came a longer sleeveless surcoat in a fine blue wool, a little paler in shade than her temporary master's cloak. Finally, a wide leather belt, with a plain circular clasp, was used to pull in and girdle her waist, and a pair of practical leather boots adorned her bruised feet.

Clothes such as these, Mathilda knew, placed her in the arena of those who worked for the rising gentry, rather than those who traded for a living. For the daughter of a potter who only just kept his family alive on his own tiny stretch of land and his skill with clay, it was a major transformation.

Mathilda curtseyed to each brother in turn, starting with the one at the head of the table, whom she assumed was John, the eldest brother and Lord of Ashby Folville. The row of candles on the table flickered in the draught of the hall, obscuring the shadows, making it difficult to accurately assess all the men's features.

'You appear much improved, Mistress Twyford.' Robert nodded encouragingly at her, but Mathilda had spotted a furrow to his brow which didn't quite match his warm tone, 'Let me introduce you to some of my family.'

Robert gestured to the head of the table. 'This is my second brother, Eustace de Folville.'

Mathilda curtseyed again, reappraising the man she'd incorrectly taken to be the lord of the manor. She judged he was already about thirty-five years of age. His stature and broad build matched that of his brother, and his attire was of the latest European style. His face was smooth, and his hair cropped short in the French fashion. Mathilda recalled how she'd heard her father telling Matthew some time ago how the Folville family had originally come over to England with William the Bastard from Picardy in France and had been entrusted with Ashby Folville as a reward for their services.

Robert moved his attention to the next chair. 'This is my brother Laurence, and next to him is my brother Richard, rector of Teigh, with whom you have already become acquainted.'

Again, Mathilda reflected that even though he'd lost the fishy aroma, Richard de Folville couldn't have appeared less like a rector if he tried. In fact, Mathilda was having trouble picturing a less pious-looking man; yet she bowed with sensible grace and acknowledged his religious status. 'Greetings, Father.'

'These are my brothers, Thomas,' Robert gestured to the clergyman's neighbour, 'and, finally, Walter.'

Mathilda bowed and curtseyed again. Not entirely sure which gesture was expected of her, so adopted a generally submissive position somewhere between the two.

Returning to his seat, Robert left Mathilda hovering, small and vulnerable, before the panel of universally blue eyes, square jaws and muscular frames. As she observed them studying her in return through the dim light, Mathilda has no problem imagining them delivering their own brand of justice; and in some cases, relishing doing so.

'You wish to know where our elder brother and Lord of the manor, John de Folville is?'

In fact, Mathilda had been wondering why Eustace, more than any other brother, exuded a controlled menace from a disconcertingly blank expression 'Yes. Forgive me if I ask too much, my Lord,' she answered Robert stoutly, but then lowered her eyes further, suddenly unsure if she had been supposed to reply.

Eustace roared with laughter and raised his ale to Robert. 'You are right, brother. The chit is a bold one.'

Mathilda's face coloured as she continued to concentrate on the dirty patch of ground between her feet. The other brothers, with the exception of Robert, joined in the thunderous laughter, but, Mathilda suspected, they laughed more out of duty then any genuine stirrings of amusement.

'I believe she is what we need, Eustace.' Robert spoke firmly. 'She is brave and has some letters.'

Eustace chewed at the inside of his cheek. 'Quick-witted as well, I'll warrant.'

'I believe so.'

'Your age, child?' the rector cut in, his question a brusque demand.

'I am nineteen, Father.' Mathilda already hated him. The others she was wary of, and Eustace she would always be afraid of, but the rector oozed a cold lack of compassion. She vowed to keep as far away from him as possible.

Richard said no more, but his hawk-like eyes never left her.

'Tell me, girl,' Eustace scowled at his cleric brother, 'do you know why it was necessary to place you in the cell?'

Mathilda glanced at Robert, checking if she was supposed to reply this time. The almost imperceptible bow reassured her. She swallowed, thinking quickly, 'I may be wrong, my Lord, and I beg your pardon if I offend, but I suspect it was to keep me out of the way while you decided what to do with me. To remind me of my place and to use my suffering to punish my father,' Mathilda hastily added another, 'my Lord,' and then returned her gaze to the floor.

The sinister air at the table lasted an uncomfortably long time. The fear which she had been so carefully controlling crept back and prickled the skin beneath her tightly harnessed hair. She didn't look up. She didn't want to see the angry expressions that her answer may have given them.

What will they do with me? Mathilda hadn't needed Robert to confirm for her that the Folvilles administered their own take on the law. There would be no sheriff or bailiff to intercede for her here. They might imprison her again, wound her, cut out her tongue for her insolence, or leave her in the hands of the rector…

As her fears became wilder and more painful, the gruff tones of Eustace de Folville cut through the expectant hush of the hall. Rather than comment on her statement, what he said next stunned her with its kindness. 'Your father and brother Matthew are safe.'

Mathilda opened her mouth to ask about Oswin but closed it again on seeing a warning glance from Robert and contented herself with just listening.

'They are at your home in Twyford, toiling to earn enough money to discharge their debt and have you returned to them.' Eustace's eyes seemed to bore into her soul as Mathilda choked back all the questions she was desperate to ask but had the common sense not to.

'Your father has made himself our debtor by his own free will, and debts must be paid. So,' Eustace took an unpleasant-sounding guttural breath as he stared at the newly scrubbed girl, 'you are our prize until your family discharges their payment.'

He walked towards the fire, warming his palms against the approaching cool of the summer evening. 'My brother Robert already speaks well of you. I see a liking there, although at nineteen you are already two years past your prime.'

Mathilda couldn't decide if Eustace was teasing her or scolding his brother and daren't glance towards Robert to see how he responded to such a comment. The rector sniggered, saying 'Past her prime is an improvement for you, Robert,' quietly into his wooden mug of ale.

Robert blanched angrily at the rector's jibe, but said nothing, as Eustace continued, 'You know something of us, Mathilda, from living in these parts. And I have no doubt, my dear brother has explained to you our beliefs on maintaining our lands and beyond, keeping a weather eye on the dealings of all men in this hundred.'

Mathilda bit her tongue in an effort to remain demurely mute, trying to concentrate on what Eustace was saying and not on the unknown fate of her younger brother.

'He has also, I believe, told you of his fascination with stories,' Eustace gave Robert a blunt stare; leaving Mathilda to wonder whether it was his brother's passion for the minstrels' tales, or the fact he'd shared that belief and interest with a mere chattel, that Eustace disapproved of.

'The balladeers have become obsessed of late with the injustices of this land. Often rightly so. Naturally the fabled Robyn Hode has become a hero. An ordinary man who breaks the law and yet somehow remains good and faithful in the eyes of the Church, is bound to be favoured. In years past such a character's popularity would have been unthinkable, but these days, well …' Eustace began to pace in front of the fire, reminding Mathilda of how his brother had moved earlier, 'Now we are empowered by the young King, the Earl of Huntingdon, and Sheriff Ingram, to keep these lands safe and well run, and by God and Our Lady we'll do it, even if we have to sweep some capricious damned souls to an earlier hell than they were expecting along the way.'

Eustace was shouting now, but not at her. His voice had adopted a hectoring passion, and Mathilda resolved that she would never willingly disappoint this man; it would be too dangerous.

'Many of the complaints of crimes and infringements that reach my family's ears are not accurate. Far more felonies are alleged out of spite or personal grievance than are ever actually committed. We require more eyes and ears, girl. Accurate, unbiased eyes and ears. The sheriff of this county is not a bad man. No worse than the rest anyway; but Ingram is sorely stretched. He has not only this shire, but Nottinghamshire and Derbyshire within his writ. The man cannot be everywhere at once. No man can.

'We are believed to have a band of criminals under our control, Mathilda. This is not true. I'm no Hode, although I am lucky to have the respect of the immediate population, and although I know that respect is because they go in fear of me, I'd rather have that than no respect at all. Hode's principles I embrace, as I do other outlaw heroes' who have flouted a law more corrupt than they are. Those such as Gamelyn can give a man a good example to follow. What was it he declared, Robert, to the Justice at his false trial?'

Moving into the light of the table, Robert thought for a second before reeling off a verse he'd probably known by heart since childhood,

'Come from the seat of justice: all too oft
Hast thou polluted law's clear stream with wrong;
Too oft hast taken reward against the poor;
Too oft hast lent thine aid to villainy,
And given judgment 'gainst the innocent.
Come down and meet thine own meed at the bar,
While I, in thy place, give more rightful doom
And see that justice dwells in law for once.'

Eustace nodded to his brother, who'd already shrunk back into the shadows of the nearest wall. 'I do not have such a band at my beck and call, Mathilda. When I need help I have to pay for it.'

While Eustace spoke, the other members of his family pointedly stared at Mathilda as they drank ale, which was frequently topped up by Allward, the servant boy who'd provided her with food earlier.

Sitting on a seat with a sigh, Eustace gestured to All-ward to add more candles to the room, for the approach of evening was filling the place with an encroaching gloom.

'To answer the question you didn't actually ask, Mistress Twyford, the Lord John de Folville is currently in Hunting-don. We are enfeoffed to them, and the connection is strong. He is often there. This manor is run, on a practical level, by the Lord Robert, who acts as steward, with additional assis-tance from the rector of Teigh here.'

Mathilda shivered, refraining from meeting the gaze of the hard-eyed man who'd dragged her from prison, mak-ing sure he touched as much of her flesh as possible, as he snorted with ill-concealed contempt from his seat on the far side of the table.

Eustace sighed nosily. 'I am telling you this because it will be important in the time ahead. You are to appear to the world to be Robert's woman.'

Mathilda couldn't disguise her sharp intake of breath at that news and ignored the smattering of smirks on the faces of the daunting panel of solidly muscular brothers before her. She hadn't really believed Robert when he'd suggested that would be her role.

'In reality you will be a gatherer of information, a de-liverer of messages. My brother, the Lord John, commands a reasonable estate which demands constant attention. I – we – need to know what is happening across its villages, holdings and beyond. I find I require someone I can trust to liaise with our colleagues in other counties. Who better than someone innocent of appearance, and whose very devotion is wrapped up in the safety of her family?'

Mathilda blinked in the face of guttering candle smoke, her throat drier than it had ever been. She was to be a spy.

This was hazardous work which warranted brutal punishments that she didn't want to think about. Mathilda forced herself to hold back her unease at Eustace's veiled threat towards her family if she refused him and listened.

'You will be the eyes and ears I speak of, Mathilda of Twyford. What say you, girl?'

There was nothing else she could say.

'Yes, my Lord.'

~ *Chapter Four* ~

From where she sat at the side of the hall, Mathilda considered her situation. She didn't really understand what they were asking of her, but she knew it was going to be dangerous. If it hadn't been then surely one of the brothers would have seen to it themselves.

Anxiously waiting on the bench in the small space that divided the hall from the kitchen door that she'd been sent to sit on, to hear details of her fate, Mathilda considered what Eustace had said. Could she be a professional tell-tale?

The fact that she'd always been good at finding things out simply by virtue of being a good listener was true; but she'd never gone out of her way to overhear things before. Gossiping really could get you into serious trouble. Not only was it frowned upon within the local towns and villages, it could lead to being arrested and punished. How would she be able to gain information of the sort the Folvilles were alluding to, without endangering herself and those innocent informers that she spoke to?

'You appear pensive, Mathilda,' Robert had emerged from the main hall, 'positively demure, even.'

Even though she suspected he was being sarcastic, Mathilda merely said, 'Thank you, my Lord.'

'I am not fooled, however. What were you thinking

about?' He surprised her by sitting beside her on the wide wooden settle.

'I was wondering how I'd get the information you require safely, my Lord.'

'You're only our messenger, Mathilda; there is no reason for you to worry about your safety.'

'Forgive me, my Lord,' Mathilda choose her words carefully, 'but I must have misunderstood. I took it that I was to be an informer for you – a spy.'

Folville almost blurted out a denial, but clearly thought better of it. For the first time he looked at her as if he'd accepted that she was no child, nor was she a fool. 'Mathilda, if you are sensible, then this is not a perilous job. Eustace laced what lies ahead of you with an exaggeration of the peril involved. It is the thing he enjoys most; making a theatre of unpleasantness and revelling in the anxiety it causes in others.'

Far from reassured by his description of Eustace, Mathilda asked, 'Do you have other messengers here, my Lord?'

Robert appeared uncomfortable, but answered her squarely, 'No; although there have been and will be again.'

Mathilda decided not to ask of the fate of the previous messenger. She had no choice in her position, and the detailed knowledge of her predecessor's death or imprisonment would not help. Anyway, she was too busy trying to work out how to tackle the other issues which preyed heavily on her mind. 'May I ask something more, my Lord?'

'You have developed a taste for questioning me, Mathilda.' Once again, the suggestion of a smile played at the corner of Robert's lips, but Mathilda remained cautious.

'I dared not ask before my Lord Eustace, but no mention has been made of my brother Oswin.'

Robert spoke candidly. 'We don't know where he is, and

that's the truth of it.'

'How so, my Lord?' Hope rose in Mathilda's chest, but she was afraid to show it too openly.

'Richard tells me Oswin slipped through his fingers by the river; fled towards Lincolnshire we think. He did not fall victim to the river. We checked for drowned men.'

Relieved to know her youngest brother wasn't lost to the water, Mathilda asked, 'Will you pursue him?'

Rising to his feet, flexing out his legs as if he was restless, Robert replied, 'No. You were our prize. Although without Oswin's help in the pottery, it will take your father longer to buy you back.'

While she digested this information, another idea began to form.

'My Lord Eustace said,' Mathilda couldn't look at Robert now; embarrassed uncertainty on her face, 'he said I was to appear as your, well, your um … companion.'

Robert sat down again, 'You fear for your reputation, girl? Your virtue? When you are already held here, when the news of you being here has probably already spread beyond the villages and into the town, placing you as a group concubine?' Robert sighed as Mathilda's green eyes focused on his, not as meek in his company as she had been. 'It is but subterfuge for your safety, Mathilda, it might cost you some blushes and some whispered remarks, but it could save your life. After all, only a desperate fool would attack the girl of a Folville brother.'

Mathilda had to acknowledge the truth of this, even if it was a truth she didn't like. In that one statement he'd as much as admitted she was open to attack after all. And yet, for all that, she felt Robert was still holding back from telling her everything.

'To that end, I have something for you.'

'My Lord?'

Reaching into the leather bag attached to his belt, Robert unrolled a delicate leather belted girdle. It was unlike anything Mathilda had ever seen and as he passed it into her hands, she ran its length through her fingers, admiring the intricacy of the work. The leather had been punched into a latticework pattern of diagonal lines and tiny butterflies, ending with a wide rectangular buckle, engraved to match the strap.

'You are supposed, in the eyes of the country, to be my woman. It is fitting for our purposes that you wear a token from me that proves our link. It will elevate you in the eyes of the world from the lips of those who enjoy spreading ill feeling and lies.'

'It's beautiful, thank you, my Lord.'

'Put it on, I want to see if it suits you.'

With fumbling fingers, Mathilda undid the belt the housekeeper had so recently forced upon her and fastened the new girdle around her waist. Smoothing it under her fingertips, turning a little so she could see it more fully, she marvelled at its beauty. 'It will be a wrench to return this, my Lord, when my job is complete.'

Roberts face blackened in anger. The abrupt change in his appearance made Mathilda step back in fear, 'It is a gift, girl, do not insult me by suggesting it should be returned.'

Mathilda spoke hastily, 'My Lord, I'm so sorry. I assumed, well ... the subterfuge and everything, my Lord. I never meant to offend, I'm truly sorry.'

He gave an almost guttural grunt, as he regarded her ashen upturned face. Speaking with the manner of a man not used to curtailing his anger so quickly, Robert was curt, 'I suppose your assumption is not strange in the circumstances. Come, you need food and rest. Tomorrow will be a long day.'

Having eaten a meal of stew and bread alone near the fire, Mathilda wasn't sure what she was supposed to do. It was late, and only Allward was up, bustling about at the other end of the hall, preparing the room for the coming of the new day, before bedding down behind the screens for a night on his straw mattress. Robert hadn't told Mathilda where to sleep, nor if she was to wait for him after she'd finished eating.

Pulling her cloak closer around her shoulders, Mathilda shuffled a few inches nearer to the fireplace. Her finger ran the length of the new girdle again in wonder. It really was beautiful, a work of art; she wondered where it had come from. She'd been worried for a while that it had been stolen, but Robert had implied it had been made especially for her, and Mathilda choose to believe that was the case.

Watching the dying flames, Mathilda decided that if Robert didn't turn up in the next few moments, she'd go and ask Allward where she should bed down for the night. While she waited, she prayed to Our Lady with every inch of her being, something, Mathilda hadn't done in earnest since the famine of a few years ago had so cruelly taken her mother from her.

~ *Chapter Five* ~

Robert found Mathilda on her knees before the fire. Her lips were moving so fast that he could hear the rush of silent words she offered gallop straight from her mouth to heaven. He marvelled at how the girl could still have faith after all that had happened to her.

The crop failures of recent years had cost the whole country so dear, and many, including Mathilda, had lost parents or children as a result. Add to that the growing failure of her father's business; her missing brother; and now, her own kidnap and enforced service; surely any one of those events alone were enough to end any faith.

Folville shook himself. Of course, she believed. Everyone believed; it was safer that way. Yet the fervour of her prayer still amazed him. Perhaps this girl wasn't so different from the rest of them after all.

Robert waited for her to finish, before making his presence known and helping a now silent Mathilda rise from the cold floor. 'I did not expect to see you appealing to the Almighty.'

'My Lord?'

'You have not had it easy, child. Praying has not helped you in the past.'

'You speak blasphemy, my Lord.' Shocked at his words

and her challenge of them, which had escaped from her lips before common sense had the chance to grip hold of her tongue, Mathilda lowered her eyes.

'And you think blasphemy, girl, I have seen it in your face.'

Indignant, Mathilda pulled her body to its utmost height, 'Did not Robyn Hode, despite his defamed state, still risk capture, arrest, death even, to reach the shrine of Our Lady in Robyn Hode and the Monk, my Lord?'

Robert failed to contain his grin 'I forgot your memory for a tale, child. You are right, he did.'

'And I think, my Lord,' Mathilda spoke almost haughtily, the realisation that, at least for now, the Folvilles needed her so were unlikely to dispose of her yet, making her braver, 'if I may speak as boldly as you say I do, that our charade will only be successful if you stop referring to me as "child".'

Folville studied Mathilda carefully once again, as if he was searching for something he'd previously missed in her expression. What was it about her that made her so brave in the face of her own peril? He didn't for a second think it was because she was foolhardy.

Gesturing for her to follow him, Robert escorted Mathilda into the side room where she'd been bathed earlier. 'Sit down, Mathilda. We have much to discuss, and we need privacy to do so.'

Wiping a bench free of her own damp clothes, that had been laid out to dry, a wary Mathilda waited for her new master to speak.

'You are going on a short journey to Bakewell, stopping at Derby on the way. Do you know the road to Derby?'

Mathilda gasped; going to Derby wasn't a short journey. It was many miles away. 'I know of it, my Lord, but I've never travelled that far.'

'You didn't think your message would need delivery within Ashby Folville? I could have taken such a missive myself.' He surveyed her with an expression of amused derision, which Mathilda found unsettling, 'The debt your family has to repay involves more than money and therefore is going to take more than a quick trip or two into town or even Leicester.'

Avoiding the mocking cast in his eyes, Mathilda asked, 'And once I'm on the road to Derby, my Lord?'

'You are to ride to Bakewell. There you will ask for audience with Nicholas Coterel.'

Mathilda's face went white, and her palms clenched together.

'I see you know this name. Tell me, how does a potter's daughter know of such a man?'

Swallowing, trying to ease the sudden dryness of her throat, Mathilda said, 'I heard the name in the spring, my Lord. I was in Leicester with my father. It was a name spoken of in hushed tones. In awe and with fear.'

'Nicholas Coterel and his brother John are not men to trifle with. Nor, however, are they men you need to fear unless you have a particular cause to do so.'

Mathilda levelled her gaze upon Robert's face. Her new, more immediate fear, made her forget her position of inferiority in the hope of receiving more information about her quest. 'I see, my Lord.'

'They are like us; my brothers and I. The Coterel family see the disintegration of our country and have taken steps to curb the worst excesses of those who abuse their positions of power too widely.'

Mathilda didn't respond to his statement and as Robert kept up his acute observation of her tiny frame and delicate features, his voice gave away a hint of uncertainty for the first time.

'I admit that John Coterel appears to have developed a taste for violence beyond the necessary. Even more so than my Lord Eustace and my not-so-reverend brother Richard. That worries me. But I tell you this in confidence.' Leaning forward, Robert spoke more slowly, 'Do you understand, Mathilda? I am trusting you to keep my confidence.'

'I'm honoured, my Lord.' Mathilda was anything but honoured. With each word Robert spoke, her shaky bravery was knocked further away, and fear screamed louder just beneath the surface of her mind.

'To you I will admit I am wary about Eustace's plan to work with the Coterels, but I think he is right in one important respect.'

'My Lord?'

'Look at yourself, girl. Who would take you for anything but an honest worker? A highly placed servant of the family, doing her master's bidding? You are the perfect candidate to carry this message.'

'So I am to appear your servant to Coterel, not your woman?' Mathilda peered down at her unfamiliar clothes. He probably had a point. 'What must I say, my Lord, when I reach the Coterels' home?'

'You'll be told in good time. Once you get there, all you have to do is pass the information on and await a reply. Then you bring it back here.'

'And then I can go home?'

'If you are successful, and the debt has been repaid, then yes.' Mathilda tried not to read anything into the fact that Robert's complexion coloured slightly, and that he avoided her eyes while he replied.

'May I ask a further question, my Lord?'

'Another one?'

'It is a practical question. How will I travel, my Lord? On foot the journey will take days and yet unaccompanied on horseback, it will appear suspicious. A girl of my status out on her own will raise questions.'

Robert studied her shrewdly and with satisfaction. 'Your question is a good one.'

Standing and stretching out his legs as if restless, Robert added, 'I see no harm in telling you the rest of the plan. I will ride with you as far as Derby, we have friends there. They will accommodate us overnight and then, the following day, you are to be taken on a cart with Master Hugo, to Bakewell, where they hold a weekly market.

'Hugo is an associate of mine who fought loyally by my side in the last Scottish war. He is a master craftsman and has a stall selling leather wares. You will slip away from the stall to the Coterels' hall, deliver the message, obtain the reply and return to the market. When you are back with Hugo, you will help him sell his goods until the end of the day. I will then bring you back here.'

Relieved not to be travelling alone, Mathilda still could not believe it was going to be as simple as Robert was making it sound. 'Please, my Lord, why cannot you or your brothers deliver the message?'

Robert sighed, 'How would you react, Mathilda, if you witnessed a member of the Folville family and the Coterel family meeting?'

'Of course. It was a foolish question. I understand, my Lord.'

And she did. Very well indeed.

Part of what Robert de Folville had told her the night before had seemed unimportant while she'd listened to his instructions. During the long, lonely, wakeful night on a cot at the edge of the main hall however, Mathilda hadn't been able to stop thinking about one particular sentence. The debt your family owes involves more than money. She'd finally given up trying to decide what Robert had meant and fallen into much-needed sleep, when she was woken by the house-keeper.

Even as she blinked into the wakefulness of dawn, a mixture of the images that had plagued Mathilda's night-time thoughts continued to haunt her.

Led through to the kitchens, she found Robert already booted and cloaked, ripping off some chunks of bread and placing them in a saddlebag for the journey.

'There are things you have to know, Mathilda. Come on, girl, get some food and ale in you and come to the stables. We have to make an early start.' Striding away, Robert called over his shoulder, 'The groom has your horse ready, don't be long.'

Mathilda gulped down some ale and tried to chew the crusty bread, but it seemed to grow in her mouth, and it took a huge act of will to swallow it. She hadn't dared tell Robert that she hadn't ridden a horse since she was a small child. She always travelled in the back of her father's cart with the pots, keeping them safe from the perils of breakage on the uneven road to market.

Hastily following her new master's retreating steps, Mathilda carried the remaining bread with her. Soon she was being hoisted into the saddle of a chestnut palfrey, which she was relieved to see was shorter than she'd feared, with kind, docile eyes. A saddle roll hung from its harness, and she stuffed the bread inside in case hunger overtook her anxiety on the ride.

As they trotted briskly out of the courtyard and onto the

quiet road west, Robert drew in close to Mathilda's side. She was hanging onto the reins and her mount's mane for all she was worth. Robert raised his eyebrows as he observed her discomfort but said nothing on the matter.

'Before we arrive, you must know that my family's collaboration with the Coterels is at best a necessity, usually a financially rewarding one. It is not an alliance based on friendship. Money does the talking when it comes to John and Nicholas Coterel, perhaps even more than it does with Eustace. They afford us harbour within the Peak District sometimes, and we return the favour when required. Now and again, we mutually agree that a local issue needs addressing, and we work together to do just that.

'Then there is the matter of your position. You are supposed to be my close acquaintance, and it will be assumed that you will be aware of the details of Belers' death and its consequences. There are always consequences, Mathilda.'

Risking a glance away from her palfrey's neck to look at Robert, Mathilda saw that his face was handsome and if it wasn't for the cruel streak that could flare up in him with no warning, she could, perhaps, truly like this man. The prospect unnerved her, and Mathilda pushed it firmly to one side. 'Indeed, my Lord.'

'That my family was involved in Belers' death is widely known. That it was Eustace who arranged it, you have probably guessed. But you should also know that I helped with the planning, as did Walter.'

Feeling his hot gaze on her, Mathilda carefully concealed her reaction, but her insides clenched as she waited for Robert to continue.

'Belers had been a thorn in the side of the barons in the region for some time. It is not necessary for you to know how the breaking point was reached, but you should be aware that we were paid to do the job by De Herdwyk and La Zouche. Remember their names, Mathilda, you will be asked for them by Coterel as proof that you come from me.'

'De Herdwyk and La Zouche.' Mathilda repeated the names back at him.

'The hunt for Belers' killers was widespread, for he was an important man. Leicestershire's sheriff at the time had no choice but to pursue us.'

'Edmund de Ashby, my Lord?'

Folville was surprised, 'You know his name?'

'Indeed, my Lord, he was the sheriff.'

'You prove your worth.' Robert pulled his impressive jet-black mount closer to her more ladylike palfrey and examined Mathilda more shrewdly as they proceeded at a steadier pace, while the sun rose to its daytime position.

'Thank you, my Lord.' Mathilda, feeling as if she was less likely to fall and hit the ground now they were travelling at a walking pace, began to survey the landscape around her. This was unknown territory to her, and the world was beginning to stir, getting ready for the working day ahead.

Whispering, keeping a watchful eye on the wakeful villagers they passed, Robert made certain they couldn't be overheard as he continued his account of the events of two years ago. 'The authorities couldn't catch us, but they had to do something to illustrate their attempts to do so, however futile. A trailbaston was held in our absence, and they took our lands in Reresby as punishment for conspiracy. And then we were outlawed.'

Mathilda drew in a sharp breath. This she hadn't known to be true. She'd heard rumours but had dismissed them. He'd been outlawed! That meant even being witnessed talking to his man put her in danger.

Seeing Mathilda's reaction, Robert said, 'Fear not, you

are not vulnerable with me. Our outlawry was lifted with a pardon a year later. My brothers and I quit the region for a while during its application. We considered our arrest and payment for a quick pardon, followed by a short time in the service of the King, worthwhile for ridding the world of a scoundrel like Belers.'

Mathilda hadn't heard the last part of what Robert had said. Her breath had snagged in her throat. An outlaw! The balladeers' songs of Robyn Hode she'd heard at the annual horse fair last year swam in her head. Robert became more like the hero of folklore with each new revelation.

'There is more,' Robert's chin was thrust forward in defiance, 'My family supported Thomas of Lancaster, a sturdy voice during the times of chaos.'

Mathilda said nothing and in truth, knew nothing of this name beyond its connection to power.

'Lancaster's supporters are not considered welcome in this new England, and I have charges hanging over me on that score, although I've never been arrested for them. Nor will I be!'

Robert sped his mount to a trot now they'd passed through the last village for a while and reached Charnwood Forest. 'That is enough for now,' he called across to Mathilda, whose palfrey was bouncing her up and down mercilessly in the saddle. 'Keep close to me through the forest. Not too fast though, or we will draw too much attention to ourselves.'

~ *Chapter Six* ~

The smell hit Mathilda long before she realised they were approaching the outskirts of Derby. As the horses turned away from the woodland, the town walls came into view, and soon Mathilda was burying her nose beneath the fold of her cloak. Her eyes began to smart as the combination of rotting meat, human waste, bones and mould from the town's stagnant waste ditch came into view and tugged unpleasantly at her senses. The stench scratched at the back of her throat as she unwisely opened her mouth to breathe while trotting past the offending feature as quickly as possible.

Riding in single file behind Robert, keeping her eyes fixed firmly on his back, not wanting to see if the people they passed were looking at her or not, Mathilda drew a silent sigh of relief as they arrived at their destination.

Stiff from the journey, Mathilda had to be bodily lifted from her palfrey by the groom waiting in the small neat courtyard which formed the entrance to Master Hugo's empire. Flexing her arms and legs, she tried to ease the ache in her limbs without drawing attention to herself.

Hanging back from Robert and the steward, who'd quickly approached him as a familiar face on their arrival; Mathilda examined the scene around her.

The courtyard was not large and from its centre she could see a narrow alleyway running off to its right, which presumably led to the stables. Directly before her was the main house. A fine, gabled building, modest in size, but superior to the standard tradesman's dwelling. Attached to the house was a workshop, behind which Mathilda could just see some strips of land sloping gently upwards, which were obviously in productive use for the household and, assuming this was a demesne property, to provide food as part of the landlord's taxes.

An overpowering smell of leather filled the air. It knocked away the lingering stench of the town ditch that had so recently invaded Mathilda's nostrils. Remembering that Robert had told her that Master Hugo was a merchant who dealt his wares far beyond the shire, Mathilda started to compare the opulent surroundings to her own home.

Mathilda's father was an excellent potter, but due to the readily available quantities of clay in the region, there were many other potters in Leicestershire. It wasn't enough to be the best any more, especially with the added pressure of foreign imports. You needed to have a head for business, and her father had always lacked that. Although it would never have been openly admitted, it had been her mother who'd quietly got on with that side of things and since her death, the difference in their fortunes had been staggering.

Mathilda's contemplation was cut short as Robert called across the yard, 'Come, Mathilda, Master Hugo is expecting us within.'

It was strange and yet reassuring to be escorted on Robert's arm into the square room which formed the main centre of activity for the house. So, thought Mathilda, our fake courtship has begun, even though we are in the home of a trusted ally. Her heart thumped in her throat as she walked demurely next to Robert, her eyes taking in the detailed tapestry that hung against the wall opposite the fire place, its rich colours reflecting heat back into the room.

Practically furnished, the house spoke of sensible expenditure. The few luxuries that were evident all had a worthwhile nature; hangings to maintain warmth, and pots and cups that had been made to last, rather than to show off with.

The man Mathilda assumed to be Master Hugo entered the room in a flurry of bustle. A servant came at his side, armed with a tray holding a pitcher and, rather tellingly, only two pewter mugs.

Mathilda's mind had conjured up the expectation of Master Hugo being a large, powerfully built, jovial man with thick red hair and huge hands. The reality of his appearance was a stark contrast to this preconceived image.

Dressed simply, but in quality cloth, Master Hugo was small of stature and slim, with thin fingers and hands that seemed to hang off the arms which were now wrapped around Robert, embracing him in a friendly greeting that lasted for an uncomfortably long time. While she didn't feel exactly threatened by Hugo's presence, as she had done when she'd met the rector of Teigh, nor was she in wary awe as with Eustace, Mathilda still found she'd taken an instant dislike to the man. Although she had no idea why.

Robert regarded Hugo with respect but said nothing. The atmosphere in the room changed as they faced each other, and even though she'd been instructed to be there, suddenly Mathilda felt as though she was intruding.

The oddly uncomfortable spell was broken by the clatter of a dropped cup. The servant muttered his apologies, which were irritably brushed away by Master Hugo as he picked up the fallen vessel and began to pour out two portions of ale.

'So Folville, this is your prize from the Twyford debt?' he said in an unexpectedly deep voice.

Mathilda flinched inwardly at being referred to in this way, but she wisely held her tongue. She realised with some shame that she had relaxed in Robert's company and for a few precious moments had forgotten the reality of her position. In the privacy of her thoughts, Mathilda swore there and then that she must never again forget that she was a mere object to these people. A tool; something to be used while they could and if she perished in the process – well, there were plenty more where she came from …

'Yes, Hugo, this is Mathilda de Twyford. A fine young woman.'

Hugo's smile didn't quite meet his eyes as he accepted her curtsy with a dismissive curl of his lips.

'Mathilda knows the plan. It only remains for me to pass on my family's message to her. Once it has been delivered, you'll be able to borrow her help to sell on the stall until the end of the day. I'm sure there will be no problems.'

'Without problems you say, Robert. Really?' Hugo's doubts were plain. Mathilda could almost feel the words that were roaming around his head. A mere woman. She'll be useless.

'Do not be mistaken by her appearance, Hugo. Mathilda is a sharp, intelligent woman, older than she appears to be. She also has a lot to lose if things don't go as we desire. She would be foolish to let us down, and I can assure you Mathilda is no fool.'

Mathilda's palms prickled with sweat. Robert spoke with a confidence that should have flattered her and perhaps it would have done, if it hadn't been accompanied with such a strong hint of menace at the prospect of her failure. All along their journey through the county roads, Mathilda had convinced herself that she would be fine and that all would be well soon. Now she was here, at this house in Derby, that confidence was wavering. Tomorrow she would have to travel a considerable distance with this Master Hugo, who obviously didn't trust her and plainly didn't even like her. A feeling that was entirely mutual.

She suspected that Robert did trust the leather worker, though – he was the most relaxed Mathilda had seen him during their short yet eventful acquaintance.

Hugo pointedly passed a cup to Robert, dismissing Mathilda with a barked request which sounded very much like an order. 'Woman, you will go to the workshop and find Mary. Until the morning, you can assist her as she wishes. There is a good deal to do before we go to market.'

Mathilda wordlessly curtseyed again and followed the inclination of Master Hugo's head, hoping it would lead her where she was bidden. Glancing back as she reached the door, she saw the two men already engrossed in conversation and paying no attention to her at all.

The workshop was small, but warm and felt much more familiar and welcoming than the main house. Mary, an able-looking woman of about five-and-thirty years, had her sleeves firmly rolled up and was hard at work piling belts into a wooden crate.

'I've been sent to help.' Mathilda spoke shyly; glad to be away from the unsettling atmosphere of the main house.

'You must be the girl from Twyford. I'm Mary and any help you could give would be very gratefully received.'

'I'm Mathilda.' It was a genuine welcome, and Mathilda took to her companion straight away.

Mary gestured a full hand towards the only other occupant of the room. 'This is Roger, Master Hugo's apprentice.'

Mathilda greeted him politely, but the lad, no more than fourteen years old, only nodded curtly in response as she passed him on her way to the far end of the workshop to help Mary with the boxes of stock. It was obvious he was learning his manners from his master as well as his trade, for he offered no further words to the two females.

Deciding to concentrate her attentions on Mary and not beyond the immediate hour, Mathilda asked, 'Master Hugo works leather?'

'Yes,' Mary pointed to Mathilda's girdle, 'that's one of his.'

Mathilda stroked the fine belt she wore in wonder, stunned that such an obnoxious little man could have made something so beautiful. As she searched about her, she saw an array of equally detailed pieces of work, many of which held the same intricate pattern of lines and butterflies. Passing each separate item in turn for Mary to pack in soft barley straw, Mathilda caressed them with the reverence such works of art were due.

'They're beautiful.'

Mary smiled. 'Indeed, my master has the gift for his craft.'

Mathilda looked up in surprise. 'Master? Forgive me, I assumed you to be his wife.'

The older woman let out a short laugh that contained no trace of humour. 'Master Hugo wants no wife.'

~ *Chapter Seven* ~

Whether it was sheer fatigue from the previous day's early start, the travelling, or the work she'd shared with Mary and the uncommunicative Roger, Mathilda slept soundly in her allotted corner of the room above the workhouse. Her body felt jolted and confused when she was a woken by Mary, who shook her to consciousness before even the crack of dawn.

'I'm sorry, Mathilda, but it's a lengthy ride to Bakewell, and you need to get there to set up before trading starts.'

Soon alert, Mathilda sat up and tried to conquer the panic that threatened to rule out all sensible thought.

She had expected Robert to come and find her yesterday, but he hadn't. She'd remained closeted away with the workers and had seen nothing of either him or Master Hugo for the remainder of the day. On the other hand, Mathilda had learnt a lot about the leather trade from Mary – how the market stall was operated, how much they charged for each item, and so on. She'd concentrated hard, understanding how important it was that she appeared to know what she was doing once she was at the market. Thankfully, the leatherworker's sales procedures were not very different from her father's potter sales technique, although the quality of his goods was far higher; as were the prices.

Mathilda barely registered the breakfast Mary forced upon her, nor did she recall, when she thought back later, either putting her clothes on or Mary helping her to dress her hair in a practical style. All Mathilda remembered, as she sat behind a pointedly silent Master Hugo, her cloak wrapped tightly around her, were the words Robert had spoken to her when he appeared on the scene just before she'd left the security of the workshop.

'You will listen to the directions Master Hugo gives you on the journey. He will tell you how to get from the market to the Coterels' manor.' Robert had gently shaken her shoulder. 'Are you listening, Mathilda?'

She'd nodded, wiping the sleep from her eyes as she swallowed some moisture down her nervously dry throat.

'Good. Once you're at the manor house, you will ask to be taken to the steward. To him and to him alone, you will say the names I gave you earlier. That is all he'll need to hear to grant you an audience with either John or Nicholas Coterel. Once you've been admitted, you will give whichever of the brothers is present Eustace's message. Are you ready to hear that message, Mathilda?'

'Yes, my Lord.'

'Right then. "De Vere has agreed". That's all it is. An easy sentence to relay.'

Mathilda repeated the words back to him and curtsied.

'Well done.' Robert examined Mathilda's her slight statute as if deciding what to do, before adding, 'There's something else.'

'My Lord?'

'I want you to have this. Just for your protection, you understand. I'm sure you won't have need of it, but these are uncertain times.' He pulled a short, sheathed dagger from the folds of his cloak and passed it to a stunned Mathilda.

'I can't carry this, my Lord. If I'm found with it, you know what they'll do …'

'Keep it hidden beneath your cloak.'

'But, my Lord, it'll be visible when I bend over.' With her milky skin growing even paler, Mathilda asked, 'Do you honestly think I'll have to use this, my Lord?'

'Keep it with you, Mathilda. For the unexpected. Not that there will be anything like that, but …'

'It's an uncertain time, my Lord, yes, you said.' Mathilda took the short blade and weighed the handle in her palm. It was a perfectly made piece, carved and patterned across the handle, with a single blue stone placed between the blade and the hilt. 'I'll conceal it beneath my outer dress. If I put another belt there, it can be slotted safely, and it'll be placed further out of sight.'

'Again Mathilda, you are wise …'

'For someone so young, my Lord? You keep speaking of me as though I am a child. Yet I am nineteen, not nine. And you are sending me into the lair of some of the most notorious men in this Hundred, on a mission you, I hope, would not lay upon a child.'

Robert smiled in rueful acknowledgement of her words, before catching Mathilda totally off guard and drawing her close and hugging her briefly. 'Be careful. Follow your orders, listen to Master Hugo, and then come back to me. I'll take you home to Ashby Folville.'

'Thank you, my Lord,' Mathilda muttered, her cheeks burning, astonished at such a gesture from the man who was essentially her gaoler. If it was meant to reassure her, it had failed, for it just reinforced the perils of what awaited her. Maybe that had been his way of saying goodbye, in case I don't make it out of Bakewell?

'You must go. Hugo is ready to leave.'

'My Lord,' Bowing briefly, Mathilda turned to go, but one more question burned in her throat so fiercely, that she had to ask, 'Forgive me, but Master Hugo? Do you trust him?'

Roberts's face flushed with anger, and for a second Mathilda flinched in readiness for an explosion of his temper, but he caught himself and in a sharp, controlled voice said, 'I would trust him with my life. Something that I have in fact done on the battlefield on more than one occasion.'

She bowed again and left without another word, wondering though if Master Hugo could be trusted as generously with her life.

An hour had passed since they'd left Derby, and although dawn was still in the process of breaking, the roads were busy. The rough grating of wagon and cart wheels bumping their way over the pitted track that led to Bakewell resounded in Mathilda's ears. Feeling Robert's knife pressing against her thigh, Mathilda wriggled into a more comfortable position in the back of the cart, pulling the thick brown travelling cloak she'd borrowed from Mary closer around her shoulders. The day promised sunshine, but the early mists had yet to clear, and the frostiness in the air was trying to burrow between her layers of clothing.

Mathilda was glad of the bustling presence of the other traders travelling the same road, for she had dreaded being alone with Master Hugo. Greetings were called and exchanged as those heading to Bakewell recognised each other from other markets and fairs. Yet Mathilda kept her own mouth shut, just in case she was spotted by someone from the markets she had frequented with her father. She didn't want to have to answer questions as to why she was there.

Sat in the back of the cart amongst the leather wares,

Mathilda closed her eyes. This spare time was dangerous – it allowed her to think. She wanted to stay busy to drive away the worries that beset her about her family. Was her brother Oswin home now, or lost in Lincolnshire? Or somewhere else entirely? Were Matthew and her father working all the hours of daylight they could to get her home, while still managing to support themselves and keep the home going?

Another thought hit her. If she jumped off the cart now, she could easily disappear into the woodland that currently bordered the road. It would take several days to get home, but she could do it, and then … no, that wouldn't help. The debt would still need paying, and the Folville brothers wouldn't be likely to stop at kidnap next time.

Banishing plans of potential escape, Mathilda bought her mind back to the matter in hand. So far, she had avoided having to talk to Master Hugo, but as they drew closer to their destination, she knew that would have to change.

Still not really sure what bothered her about Hugo so much, Mathilda sighed quietly. Although he hadn't gone as far as being friendly this morning, at least he had been courteous. She'd been treated well in his home, and he was helping her to carry out her allotted task; albeit one that she'd rather not be doing.

Yet there was something about the way he appraised her, with a sort of resentment about his features, which made Mathilda feel vulnerable and uncertain. He was a successful merchant, he was free of many of the worries the majority of the trading and lower classes had to endure; surely, she was the one who should have been resentful of him?

Her thoughts ceased as the cart negotiated the stone bridge over the River Wye, which announced their abrupt arrival at the gates of Bakewell. The wagons before them had started to form a queue, as stewards and other assorted officials directed the traders, entertainers and merchants to their allotted stalls. As they edged forward to take their turn, Master Hugo called to Mathilda. Clambering down from the cart, she took hold of the horse's bridle to lead them into the market place.

Speaking in a low mumble, Hugo said, 'Once we are set up and the earliest customers begin to arrive, that will be your best chance to slip away. But don't be long, child, by noon business will be brisk, and I require the help that was promised me.'

'What if I can't get back on time? I wouldn't want your business to suffer because of me.'

Hugo stared at her shrewdly as he explained that there was a town boy that helped him out sometimes and that they'd manage until she returned. If they had to.

Mathilda nodded. 'The directions, my Lord?'

'I am not your lord, nor anyone's.' He spat his bitterness.

'Forgive me, Master Hugo; I simply meant to show respect.'

'Indeed.' He seemed far from convinced, but after a few uncomfortable minutes he shared the information she needed.

'From my stall you must go left and walk the length of the fair; once you reach the final stand in the row you'll see two roads. Take the second on the right-hand side and follow it for about a mile. The manor you seek will be there. It is an easy route, but not an easy assignment. I confess I am astonished by Folville's choice of mate and confidante.'

Biting back the retort that came to her lips, Matilda merely said, 'Thank you, Master Hugo. I shall return as soon as I am able. I do not wish to linger with the Coterel family for any longer than I have to.'

~ *Chapter Eight* ~

Thanks to Mary's instructions and the time they'd spent in Roger's dour company, sorting the plain practical belts and aprons from Master Hugo's intricate girdles, delicate butterfly-patterned belts, and dagger sheaths, the market stall was soon set up.

The crisp morning air remained cool, but the earlier promising hint of sunshine was starting to break through, and despite her own fears, Mathilda found the buzz of happy expectation from her fellow traders was infectious. The first customers of the day were already descending upon the scene, as jugglers and other street players started to ply their light-hearted entertainment alongside the merchants of the county and beyond.

Laid out opposite a row of houses belonging to the town's richer merchants, each with their shutters open and fine fabrics, spices and even silverware on show, the market comprised a series of moveable wooden stalls that ran from one side of the square to the other. Every possible commodity was available, providing one had the money to pay for it. As well as Master Hugo's finest leatherwear at the far end of the second row of stands, there were stalls selling intricately worked pieces of jewellery, wicker baskets, combs and skeins of wool, and rolls of fabric as well as food of all varieties, from the local to the exotic.

The day seemed to be passing incredibly fast to Mathilda. Before she'd had the chance to think about planning her exit properly, the boy, Tom, had arrived to help, and the time had come to go.

Bidding them a temporary farewell and hoping to see Master Hugo again however much she didn't like him, the outlaws' hostage slipped away. With a racing heart, Mathilda raised her hood and hugged her cloak around her, afraid that Robert's knife would be spotted despite being hidden beneath several layers of clothing.

Glancing around to check no one was looking at her in particular, Mathilda allowed herself to be engulfed in the crowd of shoppers. Edging steadily closer to the last stall in the row, she spotted a priest, who had been working his way through the crowd, playing his rosary beads through his fingers as he went, and followed in his wake.

After a while, Mathilda could make out the gateway she had to pass through over the crowd's heads.Skirting the priest and passing stalls displaying apples, roasting pigs and freshly baked bread, she kept moving. Not even the acrid aroma of butchery that was floating though the market on the prevailing breeze registered as Mathilda, her palms damp with nerves, neared her goal.

Soon only two stands remained to be passed. Mathilda could see the narrow walkway ahead, between a small banked-off yard and the back wall of a workshop. She had just increased her pace, when Mathilda spotted a familiar face behind the final stall of the row.

She froze on the spot before pulling her hood further forward, covering as much as her face as possible, as she watched Geoffrey of Reresby selling his pots with comfortable ease.

A jealous, angry bile rose in her throat as her eyes ran over the mass of ceramic ware he could afford to offer. He may have appeared welcoming and friendly, but Mathilda knew differently. Reresby had beaten her father to the best pitches at markets and fairs for the past few years, often cheating or bribing his way into favour with the local lords so that they would buy from him and no one else.

She was only partially surprised to see him so far from home; this was a popular market after all. Mathilda also knew of her own father's shortcomings. It would never cross his mind to travel so far to make money.

Staying shrouded behind a group of women chatting about the goods on offer, Mathilda moved slowly with them, until at last she was close enough to the alleyway to slip away from the market without Geoffrey seeing her. Suppressing the idea of turning back to throw one of the small stones which littered the edges of the road, at the stall to smash some of his pots, Mathilda left the jollity and industry behind her; wondering if it was her presence with the Folvilles had been the cause of this uncharacteristically violent urge.

Just as Master Hugo had said there would be, a choice of roads presented themselves before Mathilda. Taking the right-hand one as instructed, she walked purposefully, trying to give out the air of someone who knew where they were going, and had a perfect right to be there.

She had travelled about a mile and had left the final dwelling behind her some time ago; yet there was no manor house in sight, just a stretch of furlongs to the right and a cluster of coppiced wood to the left. Mathilda dare not ask any of the people at work on the land for help. Anyway, the market had drawn most of the population away from their daily labours for a few precious hours, and the dusty narrow lane before her lay unusually deserted. Suddenly, now she allowed herself to think, Mathilda felt unsafe and intimidated.

Slipping between the semi shelter of the trees she came to a standstill, her mind racing. Somehow, she must have gone wrong. Thinking fast, she reran her instructions through her head. *Go on the right path and keep going.* She had done exactly that.

Childish tears sprang to the corners of her eyes. She scrubbed them away, angry at herself, but angrier with Robert. He'd trusted Master Hugo, even though she hadn't. There was no other conclusion to reach. The leatherworker had given her the wrong directions on purpose.

A vision of her father and brothers flashed through Mathilda's mind. She wouldn't let them down. For that matter, she didn't want to let Robert down either. Not because she cared about him, she told herself, but because she wanted to prove she wasn't the little girl he thought she was. And moreover, she wanted to prove she was worthy of the expectations of his family as well as her own. Although the Folvilles' methods worried her, they were effective, and the fear they engendered was at least mixed with respect. Not like Master Hugo!

'What would Robyn Hode do?' Mathilda whispered to herself as she crouched between the spindly trees, watching for any other sign of life. 'He'd make a plan and stick to it. I have to find the manor, so I'll have to ask someone. I have no choice. But I need a plausible reason for asking.'

This was less easy to think up. She had no money with her, so she couldn't buy a gift to pretend to take to the Coterels' home, she only had her message. Would that be enough? Or was she supposed to keep the fact she was delivering a message a secret, along with the message itself?

It had to be the gift idea. A present from a master to Coterel perhaps? A master she would have to make up, so if she was asked more details, she at least sounded plausible. How about Master Hugo? She owed him some trouble after all.

Mathilda felt the knife against her side, thankful now that Robert had forced it upon her, and with a heavy sigh strode back the way she'd come. There was only one thing she could claim was a gift to the Coterels from Master Hugo.

With a heavy heart, she undid her girdle and laid it across her palms. With any luck she wouldn't have to part with it once she'd reached the manor. She really didn't want to face Robert's fury if she lost the girdle, even if it was through no fault of her own. She ran her fingers over the pattern and was struck with the idea that she'd seen it somewhere else as she began to walk faster, her heart thudding in her chest.

Retracing her steps, Mathilda mused as to Master Hugo's motives. Why send her the wrong way? She was sure he hadn't done it by mistake. Was he really on the Folvilles' side? Or was his friendship to Robert fake on his part; the bond they forged on the battlefield merely convenient for his own plans? Mathilda resolved to be even more wary and also to say nothing to him of his success in misleading her when she got back to his stall. There was no way she'd give him the satisfaction and was determined to frustrate Master Hugo by somehow succeeding in her mission.

On reaching the first holding on the edge of the town, Mathilda called out, trying to keep the nerves from her voice, 'Excuse me.'

She was relieved when it was a child, ragged, but from labour rather than the extreme poverty of the urchins you saw in every town's main streets, who came forth at her call. 'Can I help you, my Lady?'

My Lady? Mathilda was momentarily stunned by the address, until she remembered her new attire, and quickly adopted what she hoped would be the mannerisms to go with her assumed status.

'I have taken a wrong turn, I think. My Lord has instructed me to take this gift to the manor of the Lords Coterel, do you know the way?'

The boy, who she guessed was about ten years old, shrank back as he spoke. 'The Coterel manor, you say?'

'Please. They are expecting this, I bought it from the market,' she showed the boy the girdle, 'and I fear it would be unwise to delay in its delivery.'

'You are right there, my Lady. My father says the Coterels are not patient men.' He bit his lip suddenly, as he wondered if he'd spoken out of turn.

Mathilda smiled to reassure him. 'You can direct me?'

'I can, my Lady; you are two miles adrift. Go towards the market place, and just as you reach it, there are two further paths, one to the market, and one to the left. Take the left road. A mile or so down there and you'll reach the house.'

'Thank you,' said Mathilda with all the authority she could muster.

'Please, my Lady,' said the boy as she turned to go, 'where are your horse and servant?'

Mathilda hadn't been ready for this question. After an initial pause, her words came out too quickly to be believable. 'My maid is helping at the market, and my horse is lame.'

She hastened away, uneasy at leaving the boy staring after her in disbelief, but glad that she now knew where she was going. She strode as quickly as was seemly, aware that she was already well behind time if she was to return to Hugo's stall by midday.

After a few minutes a sound behind made Mathilda turn around abruptly. It was the boy, driving a pony and cart. 'May I assist you, my Lady? I can give you a lift as far as the market, if you don't mind travelling in the cart. I'm sorry, I should have offered before.'

Mathilda only hesitated for a second before agreeing and thanking her helper.

The boy chatted away as they rode down a street which fast became narrow, and overhung with rowan and ash trees, making it hard work for the sun to penetrate through the leaves to, maintaining the ground as a sticky clay. 'I wouldn't want anyone to get any trouble from the Coterels, my Lady. I have seen them at work. No, I wouldn't want a pretty lady like you in trouble with them!'

Mathilda almost asked him what he'd seen, but then decided she didn't want to know. As they reached the crossroads she'd been at earlier, she alighted.

'Our Lady's blessings on you.'

'Thank you, my Lady. Good luck.'

This time the directions were correct, and it wasn't long before Mathilda could see the small manor house at the end of a rough driveway.

Re-securing the girdle around her waist, relieved that she hadn't had to bargain with it after all, Mathilda lowered her hood. Hovering behind an oak at the gateway, taking care not to step back into the waste pit, which had clearly been recently bedded down with handfuls of straw, so the stench was not too severe, she decided what to do next.

Nerves swam haphazardly in her stomach. These were men to be cautious of but, Mathilda thought with sudden pride, she'd already survived being kidnapped and put in the Folvilles' cell, so she could survive this. She had stood before the Folville family, and was now being trusted with a mission which, Robert had told her, was vital to them, and to the second felonious family she was about to encounter. She could do this. She must.

Judging that there must only be about an hour left until noon, Mathilda knew it was unlikely she would be back before the specified time. That was a shame; she would love to have seen the look on Master Hugo's face if she had.

Wasting no more time, and with a quick stroke of Robert's dagger for luck, she went cautiously forward.

~ *Chapter Nine* ~

The driveway wasn't long and Mathilda soon found herself within a neat courtyard.

A boy hurried up to her. 'May I help you, mistress?'

'I am instructed by my master to speak to the steward.'

Thankfully unfazed by her request, the boy ran towards what Mathilda took to be a workshop of some sort in the far corner of the yard without further comment.

She had barely time to examine her surroundings, when a gruff barrel of a man strode impatiently towards her. She'd obviously disturbed him from his labours, and he wasn't bothering hiding that he wasn't too impressed by that fact.

Mathilda spoke quickly, 'My apologies for the disturbance. You are the steward?'

'I am.'

'I have a message for you. La Zouche and De Heredwyk.'

The solid man's eyebrows knotted together in a frown of disapproval as he stared at her with disdain. Mathilda raised her chin in response, copying the expression of haughty annoyance she had seen on Sarah the housekeeper when she'd struggled to bathe her two days ago.

Grunting, 'You'd better come with me then,' the steward set off towards the main house

Following him, Mathilda resisted the temptation to run to keep up with his fast paced strides. She repeated the message over and over in her head, hoping that her welcome would be tolerated calmly, even if it wasn't well received. Most of all, she hoped the visit would be swift.

'Wait.' The steward pointed to the floor where Mathilda stood and left her in a narrow corridor between the main door and the hall. It was a larger house than at Ashby Folville, but no warmer or lighter, and as Mathilda peered around her, she saw it was in need of more care than the Folvilles home.

'Oi, in here, woman!' The steward spoke abruptly, stabbing his finger towards the hall with a dirty, calloused hand.

Going the way she was directed, into a hall busy with servants at one end and a rectangular table near the fire place at the other, Mathilda struggled to push down the sound of her blood pounding in her ears as she saw who awaited her.

A stocky man with tamed curly black hair and a clipped beard was watching her expectantly through thin dark eyes. His fine clothes told her he was a Coterel, but not which one.

'My Lord,' Mathilda curtseyed, 'I have a message.'

'Give it, child.'

'Please, my Lord, I have been instructed to ask whom I am addressing first.'

The man smiled, not a friendly smile, but a knowing smile. One that told her he would have instructed a messenger of his own to behave in the same manner should the roles have been reversed.

'I am Nicholas Coterel. The message?'

'De Vere has agreed.'

Coterel's shrewd expression gave little away, but his eyes flashed for a second with what Mathilda hoped was satisfaction. He stood stock still for a second before saying, 'You may give the Folvilles my reply. Tell them, "The message is well received. Three days. Midnight."'

'The message is well received. Three days. Midnight.'

'Exactly right,' Coterel gestured for Mathilda to sit down as he took a draft from the tanker he held, 'I am curious at Folville's choice of envoy. Who are you, child?'

Sitting as bidden, she swallowed nervously, wishing that everyone would stop referring to her as a child. Hoping she sounded convincing, she said, 'I am companion to Robert de Folville, my Lord. My name is Mathilda.'

Coterel choked on his drink, sending a fine spray across the table. 'Are you? Are you indeed? Now that is interesting …' His voice trailed off, but his eyes never left his visitor.

Mathilda stiffened, unsure how to respond, so simply said, 'If you'll forgive me, my Lord, I must return to my duties, I have another errand awaiting me.' Her eyes scanned the hall; she had an increasing feeling that Nicholas wasn't the only one watching her.

'Of course, but have a drink first; you have travelled far and must be tired. My steward tells me you have no horse. Folville did not send you on foot, I hope?'

Mathilda inclined her head with gratitude as she was presented with a cup of honeyed ale, but she didn't have the chance to reply, for Coterel hadn't finished speaking.

'I should advise you to tell me the truth, Mathilda. I suspect your young man told you all about me. Although something about you makes me believe you would never be so stupid as to lie to me anyway.'

Doing her best to ignore the sensation of the hairs standing up on the back of her neck, as well as her strengthening conviction that she was being surveyed from some hidden location in the smoky hall, Mathilda saw the sense in telling

Nicholas Coterel everything about her day so far, although how she came to be in the company of the Folvilles in the first place she kept to herself.

Coterel didn't appeared particularly shocked by Master Hugo's behaviour; although he held back from venturing an opinion as why the leatherworker might have acted in the way he had, beyond saying 'Master Hugo is an odd one and no mistake. I can see why you'd wish to get back to him on schedule. He'd hate that! It'll quite ruin his day if you succeed. I bet he's been relishing the chance to complain about you to Robert since daybreak.'

'Then I fear I'll be making his day. I can't possibly back in time, my Lord. I'm weary from walking, and it's another two miles back to the marketplace.'

Coterel regarded the messenger with open curiosity. 'Were you not scared, to walk into this notorious den of thieves?'

Mathilda again chose honesty as the best course. 'I was scared, my Lord. But it was important to Robert that I succeed.' She did not add that it was even more important to her father and her brothers.

'You genuinely have a liking for Robert de Folville, don't you?'

Mathilda found herself blushing at the suggestion, but determined to keep up the pretence said, 'He is a good man, my Lord.'

'Despite his deeds?' Coterel cocked his head to one side, a mischievous curve to his lips.

'His deeds are for the general good, my Lord.'

'Not always...'

'No, I suppose not; but often they are.' Folding her palms in her lap, it came as a revelation to Mathilda to realise that she did like Robert and was now only beginning to see it.

Nicholas broke away from his piercing appraisal of the messenger, 'I have a proposal for you. A way to dissatisfy that upstart Hugo. Are you interested?'

Mathilda leaned forward conspiratorially. 'Yes, my Lord.'

'I will lend you a mount and a lad to accompany you. If you gallop the first mile and trot the second through the town's outskirts, you ought to just about make it on time. Hugo will be dumbfounded.'

'You'd do that for me, my Lord? I'm only a messenger.'

'You are a polite and efficient emissary from the closet thing this family has to an ally in these treacherous times. Besides,' Nicholas stood up decisively, 'I can't stand that Hugo, even if his craftsmanship is second to none.' He gestured to her girdle with a wave of his hand as they walked. 'That was a present from Robert?'

'Yes, my Lord.'

'Makes sense. He won't have a word said against the belt-maker; I believe Hugo saved his life when they were in arms. My advice to you, therefore, is to keep Hugo's betrayal a secret from your suitor if you can. Robert would not thank you for doubting where he places his loyalty.'

Striding through the hall at an even faster pace than his steward had done, Nicholas forced Mathilda to jog after him. She felt oddly flat of a sudden. She'd been bursting to tell Robert about Master Hugo's lack of worth and felt disappointed that she'd been warned against it. While she considered Coterel's counsel, she peered from side to side, trying to catch a glimpse of the set of eyes she was sure had been boring into the back of her neck since she'd set foot in the hall, but saw nothing.

Once they reached the courtyard, Coterel called for his steward to make swift arrangements to ferry Mathilda to the town. 'Do you ride well, Mathilda?'

'No, my Lord, I'm afraid not.'

'Then it'll be best if you share a horse.'

He turned to a slim lad who'd emerged from the work-shop. 'You will take the Lady Mathilda to the edge of town. Leave her at the market crossroads, before riding directly back here.'

The young man inclined his head in a surly manner that reminded Mathilda of Hugo's apprentice, Roger.

Coterel himself helped Mathilda into the saddle before the lad came up behind her. It was strange having a male body pressed up against her back that didn't belong to one of her brothers, and stranger still when he wrapped his arms around her to reach the reins. A flush started at her neck as she found herself wishing it was Robert behind her. A thought she shook away as Nicholas spoke.

'Good luck, Mathilda. I shall enjoy hearing all about the countenance on Master Hugo's face when next we meet.'

Mathilda smiled down at him from the horse and found she hoped that they did meet again. 'Thank you, my Lord. I appreciate your kindness.' As she spoke, Mathilda sudden-ly remembered that Nicholas Coterel was a murderer and, some said, a rapist, and yet she didn't feel the same sense of fear and unease as she did in the presence of Master Hugo.

The lad swung the mount around and was steering them towards the gateway, when Coterel called after them. He ran back to her and put a restraining hand on her stirrup. 'Do you have a weapon? Did Robert give you his dagger?'

Mathilda was surprised. 'Why yes, my Lord, he did.'

'While you remain with Hugo, keep it close. He has no humour and may not take kindly to being thwarted, howev-er much it might amuse you and I. Take care.'

Calling back her thanks, Mathilda held onto the horse's

mane for all she was worth as Coterel's lad spurred the mount forward from a gentle walk to a full gallop in only seconds. Her mind was too full of Coterel's warning for her to even think about her dislike of riding.

It took hardly any time to reach a stream of people moving away from the market. As the horse slowed to a trot, Mathilda surveyed the myriad of wares the local populace were carrying to their various homes or places of employment. Her eye fell on a serving girl carrying a large grey pitcher. She was walking gingerly, as though her very existence depended on getting the vessel back in one piece; Mathilda supposed that it very well might. It had a familiar pattern on it. Diagonal lines, interspersed with the occasional butterfly.

The lad reined in the horse to a stop at the side of the road and helped Mathilda down.

Ignoring the curious glances of passers-by, Mathilda thanked her companion.

'My Lady,' politely inclining his head, he circled the mount around and returned the way he'd come, leaving Mathilda free to stride through the thick crowds.

Side stepping the rivulets of water and offal that were trickling from the side alleys into the main street beneath the feet of the shoppers and traders alike, Mathilda reflected that Master Hugo had been correct about the market; things were much busier now the sun had reached its height.

Even if she lived for a hundred years, Mathilda would never forget Master Hugo's expression on her safe return.

She took a secret delight in watching as he struggled to place an expression of relieved pleasure onto his weasel face, as Mathilda weaved through the stalls towards him, reaching him just as the church bells chimed twelve. It was

the sweetest feeling. A tiny victory against a man she suspected had the capacity for more danger and deception than
all the Coterels and Folvilles put together.

'I hope I haven't kept you too long, Master Hugo.'

Mathilda kept her voice demure and, without giving him
time to comment, she joined the leatherworker behind the
stall and began attending to his customers.

~ *Chapter Ten* ~

Robert barely grunted his acknowledgement of her as he watched the largely empty cart arrive back at the workshop in Derby. Mathilda hadn't expected a major display of gratitude, but the lack of a 'well done' on seeing her return alive, or a quick glance to make sure she was in one piece, hurt more than Mathilda liked to admit.

As Master Hugo's apprentice tugged Mathilda from the cart, hoisting her directly onto her palfrey for the ride back to Leicestershire, Robert disappeared into the workshop with the leatherworker. Then, only a few minutes later, his expression thunderous, he mounted his horse and impatiently gestured for Mathilda to follow him in an agitated trot out of the courtyard, without giving her the chance to eat, relieve herself, or say goodbye to Mary.

The early evening's journey from Bakewell back to Derby after the close of the market had been frosty. Master Hugo had sat morosely at the reins of the cart, despite having had a successful day's trading. Mathilda had been glad of his silence, keeping Nicholas Coterel's warning words in mind, her hand as near as she possible to Robert's secreted dagger.

Robert's silence as they returned to Ashby Folville, on the other hand, was unnerving and seemed to seethe with ingratitude. Mulling over the reply to the she'd been given by Coterel, Mathilda wondered if she should ask Robert if he wanted to hear what it was straight away. However, his sullen nature was making her nervous, and she began to consider the possibility that Master Hugo's account of her behaviour while working on his stall had been less than accurate.

A dab hand at selling, Mathilda had quickly endeared herself to the customers. She'd managed to persuade several of the merchants who came to the stand, whose fine clothing indicated they could well afford it, to purchase rather finer and more expensive goods than those they'd originally come for.

Only once had Mathilda shied away from a sale, and that was when Geoffrey of Reresby had hovered near the stall for a few seconds. The potters hawk-like gaze had lingered over Hugo's goods with an avaricious gleam that she suspected had nothing at all to do with working out how he could profit from another trader's success. Unfortunately, Hugo had spotted Mathilda moving back from a customer in order to avoid Geoffrey spotting her. He had not been pleased.

Mathilda had tried to explain the reason for her action to Master Hugo, indicating how it would not be in Robert's favour for Geoffrey to see her there, but her pleas had fallen on deaf ears. He had been far too delighted at having an excuse to admonish and belittle her in public to listen to reason.

Now, as they rode harder than necessary, she supposed Hugo must have focused on that one moment of dissatisfaction, rather than reporting to Robert how much profit Mathilda had made for him today. With her bottom bruised from bouncing out of sync with the movement of the mount, and her palms dry from a day of dealing with leather, Mathilda ached all over. She'd survived her encounter with the Coterel's and a day with the obnoxious leatherworker. Now all she had to do was to work out a way to be allowed to go home.

It didn't help that it was getting darker, and Mathilda kept peering into the trees on either side of them, constantly expecting someone to leap out at them. The dagger's hilt dug into her side, its stone bruising her thigh as she clung to the palfrey's mane. Leaning forward to help her keep her balance, Mathilda began to wonder how fast she could pull the weapon from its hiding place if they were assailed by outlaws. Then again, not even an outlaw would be stupid enough or desperate enough to attack a Folville. Mathilda didn't know if that thought gave her comfort or not, especially when she remembered that he was, or at least had been, an outlaw himself.

Forcing herself to concentrate on watching Robert's back, through windblown hair which had escaped from the linen that should have been holding her plaits in place, Mathilda reflected on how different their return journey was. On the way, Robert had stayed by her side and chatted politely. He'd made sure she was safe, that she was comfortable, and that she was prepared for what was awaiting her. Now she'd delivered the Folvilles' message his solicitousness was a thing of the past. Perhaps it had never existed in the first place but was just the way the Folvilles acted to ensure they got what they wanted.

When they finally rode through the gates of the Folville manor house, the stable boy helped Mathilda's stiff body down from her steed, his brow furrowing as he held her shivering frame upright against his. 'Are you all right, miss?'

'Thank you. I'm just a bit cold, and it has been some time since I ate.' Mathilda glanced around her. Robert had disappeared.

Uncertain which way to go and feeling unsteady on her feet, she held onto the horse, unwilling to let go of its reins least she fall to the floor. Mathilda was about to ask the stable boy where she should wait, when he gestured towards the back door of the kitchen, 'I think Sarah wants you.'

Mathilda turned to see the housekeeper tutting impatiently.

'Come on, girl!' Sarah snapped under her breath, 'the men are waiting for you!'

Passing the reins to the stable lad, Mathilda moved toward the housekeeper. Each step was an effort. She wasn't sure if she'd heard Sarah muttering about how foolish Robert was for not stopping at an inn for the night, or if she'd imagined it. Her stomach was growling so loud in protest at its lack of sustenance that it would have driven out most sounds anyway. The cold shivers that had engulfed her on the journey home were beginning to be joined by streaks of heat, and before Mathilda could call out in distress, her legs gave out from under her, and she sank with no grace whatsoever onto the damp hay-strewn gravel.

There had been a brief sensation of falling, and that the world was spinning. Darts of a sickly green hue had flashed behind her eyes. Mathilda had a vague recollection of hearing a woman shouting, and she knew male hands had lifted her from the ground and carried her into the kitchen, but she wasn't sure whose they'd been.

Now, with one of the horse's blankets swathing her, Mathilda's eyes came back into focus. She couldn't stop the quiver in her legs, and her head thudded. Doing her best to pull herself together, angry with herself at having swooned like some sort a feeble princess in front of members of the Folville household for a second time, Mathilda was about to apologise when the housekeeper let fly.

'What in heaven's name do you think you're playing at, girl? Sarah rolled up her sleeves as she spoke, and for one second Mathilda had the impression that she was going to hit her.

Sarah merely grunted in disapproval. As the world came back into a sharper focus Mathilda noticed that the house-keeper's hair hung loose around the shoulders as if she'd been preparing to turn in for the night when the returning party from Derby had disturbed her. 'Come on! They're waiting!'

Wiping dust and small shards of gravel from her palms, Mathilda struggled to concentrate. 'Sorry, Sarah. Who is waiting?' Her vision swam again, and dots of perspiration appeared on her forehead.

It didn't matter that she'd survived a meeting with Nich-olas Coterel to Sarah, who stood there like a disgruntled matriarch, with her hands on her ample hips, Mathilda was clearly as welcome as an infestation of mice in a bake house, and every bit as inconvenient.

'My Lord Eustace and his brothers, naturally!' Sarah stamped her foot impatiently, 'Heaven help us! Don't say your fall has knocked the wits from you.' Then, in a tone that was more concerned than annoyed she added in a whis-per, 'You haven't forgotten the message, have you?'

The unexpected concern on Sarah's face brought Mathil-da up short. 'You know of my errand?'

'Of course. The brothers trust me. Now,' Sarah passed Mathilda a cup of ale, 'drink this quickly, and I'll take you through.'

Mathilda stood for a minute or two, letting gravity plant her feet firmly on the ground before she attempted to move. 'I'm very sorry, Sarah. Despite recent evidence to the contrary, I am not given to fainting. I am quite all right now. Thank you for taking care of me.'

Sarah raised an eyebrow but said nothing as Mathilda pushed her shoulders back and began to walk; giving the world the firm impression that she was a woman very much in control.

Feeling far from in command of her body however, Mathilda hoped that the brothers would not keep her long, for she feared that if she didn't sleep soon, she would disgrace herself further.

~ *Chapter Eleven* ~

Swallowing the bile that swam at the base of her throat, Mathilda didn't know where to look as she was standing before the table in the main hall, at which sat all the male members of the family, including the previously absent John.

There was no doubt that the pecking order had changed now the eldest brother was in residence. Eustace's disgruntled expression said as much, even without the corroborating evidence of the uneasy atmosphere and the generally hostile body language. Mathilda wasn't sure if this was being directed towards her, or if it was a show of bravado from the younger brothers to the head of their household, which was a position only achieved by accident of birth.

Mathilda had other things to worry about. Like staying upright and not showing any weakness in front of the assembled group.

'My brothers have informed me of the reason for your presence in my home.' John's tone was so sharp Mathilda could almost feel it cutting into her. 'I would be obliged if you would prove to me that the risks taken in sending out a hostage to relay a vital message have been worthwhile. Frankly, I was amazed you returned.'

Mathilda was vaguely aware of Robert staring at her.

The expression of displeasure on his face made John's evident annoyance seem insignificant, making her wonder why she hadn't run away after all.

'So,' John tapped his dagger on the table impatiently, and Mathilda noticed that it was almost identical to the one she had hidden beneath her tunic. But for the colour of the stone it could be mistaken for the same weapon. 'The message from the Coterels? I assume you got it?'

'I did, my Lord. It was my Lord Nicholas Coterel I spoke with.' Mathilda clenched her toes inside her boots and concentrated on not letting her eyes swim out of focus.

'And? Come on, girl, what was the response?'

'He said, "The message is well received. Three days. Midnight."'

The glow of the fire behind the table was making Mathilda's eyes water, and now her mission was fully complete and the message delivered, she could feel her body shutting down again, as if it was refusing to take the instructions from her brain telling her to stay on her feet. Luckily, an arm came to her elbow, before the ground had the chance to reclaim her.

'Forgive the interruption, my Lords,' Sarah bowed with her usual sharp respect, 'but if you have finished with this girl, I require help in the kitchen to prepare for tomorrow.'

Without giving the brothers the chance to respond, Sarah steered Mathilda to the side of the hall behind the servants' dividing tapestry and sat her on the straw cot she'd rested on before.

Frowning with confused gratitude, Mathilda opened her mouth to say thank you, when the housekeeper put a finger over her lips and spoke in a guarded whisper, 'Nothing you can say to them tonight will please them. When was the last time you ate?'

'But…'

Sarah shook her head sharply, shoved a hunk of fatted bread into Mathilda's shivering hands, and placed a cup of hot broth on the floor next to her. 'Don't you get it, girl? It's not safe to talk tonight. Eat that and then sleep. I will come and find you in the morning.'

The housekeeper disappeared back into the hall as Mathilda dug her teeth into the supper that Sarah had kept warm for her; astonished that the older woman had taken the trouble to rescue her from the brothers' suspicious glances.

As Mathilda chewed, she could hear Sarah's boots crossing the stone floor and then the sound of her offering ale to the men.

The dagger handle digging into her ribs alerted Mathilda to the weapon she still carried. Not wanting to sleep with it on her person for fear of stabbing herself in the night, Mathilda pulled it from its hiding place and placed it carefully under her cot, ready to return it to Robert as soon as she had the chance.

The uncomfortable stillness that emanated from the other side of the curtain was abruptly broken by John, who either didn't realise Mathilda could hear him, or simply didn't care. 'Do we trust that this is a genuine message? What was to stop the girl making up a message so that she didn't have to face Coterel and could worm her way to freedom, and secure the safety of her family?'

Behind the tapestry, Mathilda blanched. It had never occurred to her that they wouldn't believe she had delivered an honest response.

'What say you, Robert? Eustace tells me you are soft on the girl. A fact that comes as a relief to us all, I have to say!'

Mathilda's body tensed as she waited for Robert's response. She'd thought he liked her. Or at least that he understood her need to please him to ensure her family's safety, but Robert's behaviour after their meeting with Master Hugo had given Mathilda serious second thoughts about his motives for being kind to her earlier on.

'The girl is a brave one. I have no doubts she went to Coterel as instructed. After all, the risk involved with the discovery of feeding us misinformation would be high indeed. However, we would be wise to remain cautious. The chit is unusually clever.'

Eustace spoke for the first time, 'You think that she may have sided with Coterel?'

'That is not what I am saying,' Robert snapped, 'I am merely reminding everyone present that we should never completely trust anyone involved in this venture.'

A tiny flutter of hope stirred inside Mathilda. Had Robert realised where she was, and that she could hear him? Was it him that had instructed Sarah to get her out of the brother's presence as quickly as possible? Was he addressing her in her hiding place as much as his family?

'I believe that Mistress Twyford wants to secure the freedom of her family, and that she fully understands that there are no shortcuts to that goal. If however, she does double-cross us, then she'd be extremely unwise. A fact I made very clear to her, and that I'm sure she understands.'

Mathilda almost choked on her mouthful of bread. He did know she was listening.

John virtually growled at Robert in exasperation. 'So, do you trust her in this or don't you?'

Mathilda held her breath as she waited for Robert's answer.

Robert however, did not get the chance to answer, for Eustace cut across his elder brother. 'Forget the girl, John. She got the message, and as it is pretty much the response we expected, I think we can assume it to be genuine. The real questions here are not if the girl is to be trusted, but are we ready to proceed in three nights' time with planning this necessary enterprise, and what are we going to do with the wench now?'

If Mathilda had been listening carefully before, now her ears positively strained. She'd done what they wanted; surely they were going to send her home to help her father earn enough to pay off his debt now?

Wishing she could see what was going on, Mathilda was perturbed by the ominous quiet from behind the thick curtain. She hadn't heard any footfalls, so the men must all still be there. She pictured Robert shushing them; quietly reminding his brothers that she was in the room. Or perhaps they weren't speaking because the answer to Eustace's question was so obvious to them that it only required a gesture indicating that her throat should be cut?

Despite her hunger, Mathilda found she could no longer swallow the bread. Not wanting to hear anything else, good or bad, she lay on the straw cot and pulled the thin blanket over her, trying to drown out all thoughts of her immediate future.

~ *Chapter Twelve* ~

Waking with a start, Mathilda's insides contracted in alarm to find Robert's looming body shaking her to consciousness, his palm pressed firmly over her mouth to stem the temptation to cry out.

Without time to decide if he was about to silence her forever or draw her into his confidence, Mathilda was herself tugged bodily from the cot and manoeuvred into the kitchen, still dressed in only a shift.

Taking one glimpse at Mathilda's dishevelled state, Sarah tutted loudly. 'Honestly, my Lord Robert. You can't bring the girl in here undressed. What will people think?"

'I thought that was the point!' Robert looked cross and uncomfortable as he pushed Mathilda towards Sarah. 'She's supposed to be my woman, isn't she? You said it would be a good idea.'

'It is a good idea!' Ignoring his petulant tone, Sarah took off her shawl and wrapped it around Mathilda's shoulders. 'But you are brother to the Lord of the Manor! You have to be seen to do these things with at least some level of propriety!'

Mathilda's thoughts somersaulted. What the hell was going on? Why was Sarah talking to Robert as if she was his equal? And why had Robert manhandled her here in the first place?

Before she could ask, Sarah called across the room to the lad who appeared to do every odd job about the place. 'Allward!'

Everything that was happening seemed to be going on without there being any need to have dragged her from her bed.

'Allward, go and fetch Mathilda's clothes. Quickly!' Having sent the boy on his errand, Sarah turned her attention from the occupants of the kitchen and began busying herself with getting breakfast ready for the household.

Sitting next to Mathilda on the bench by the door, Robert laid a hand on her knee, only to be visibly affronted as she hastily shoved it away again.

Shocked at herself, Mathilda opened her mouth to apologise, knowing that if she'd pulled away from him in company then she'd have been in for a mouthful of admonishment. 'I'm so sorry my Lord, I ...'

'No, Mathilda, I'm the one who should be sorry.' Robert glanced towards Sarah's back, knowing she was listening even if she wasn't watching. 'There is much to explain, and no time to explain it in.'

The early morning chill of the kitchen was making Mathilda shiver, and she was cross with herself for doing so, even though it had nothing to do with any weakness on her part, but with the fact that she'd been continually cold, hungry, or tired since she'd been deposited into the Folville home. Rather than comment and risk saying the wrong thing, Mathilda bit her tongue as she waited for Robert's explanation.

'First, I must apologise for not being able to congratulate you for your bravery in meeting with Coterel. Time was of the essence, and for reasons I am unable to divulge, it was important that I was not seen to be pleased with you.'

Frowning, Mathilda wondered if perhaps Robert distrusted Master Hugo as much as she did after all. Even as she thought about it though, she found the notion didn't ring true. There was something about the way the men were together that was too comfortable to have any level of distrust within it, and yet …

Mathilda's musings were interrupted by Allward returning with her borrowed dress, belt, and an extra shawl, which she assumed Sarah had instructed him to find for her. She expected Robert to avert his eyes while she dressed, but as Sarah rather crisply pointed out when she saw Mathilda's reluctance, he'd been sitting next to her in her shift for ten minutes, so there was little reason left for decorum now.

Dressing fast, more in her keenness to be warm than to hide the outline of her figure, Mathilda lifted the belt Robert had entrusted to her and weighed it in her hands, aware of Robert's green eyes on her as she fastened it around her waist.

'You like that belt, don't you.'

'It is most beautiful. I will be sad to give it up when I leave.' Hoping that, even if her comment made him cross again, Robert would pick up on her mention of leaving, Mathilda smoothed out her dress and sat back down.

Robert didn't rise to the opening but continued with his previous discourse. 'My brothers were pleased with the message but …' he peered about him as if checking that no one but those already in the kitchen was in earshot, 'they are cautious. You are the hostage for a debt. They have no reason to show you trust.'

'Surely the fact that I am a hostage means they should trust me. I love my family, and I want them to be safe.'

'Not all hostages care about the people who have put

them into danger in the first place.'

Mathilda only just managed to stop herself from snapping out her response. Instead, speaking with controlled calm, she said, 'I am not most people, my Lord, and now that I've done as requested I'd like to go home so I can help my father make back the money he owes you.'

Robert's expression was one of pure disbelief. 'You didn't think you'd be allowed to leave before the debt was repaid, did you?'

Feeling foolish, Mathilda's eyes flicked from Sarah to Allward, who was busy pouring ale into flagons, and back to Robert. Her voice was small when she finally managed to speak. 'But you said …'

'I told you what I was supposed to tell you. Come on, Mathilda, you're cleverer than that. You didn't think you'd get out of here so easily, did you?'

'Easily?' Mathilda felt injustice fill her up from her toes, until it was forcing itself up her throat and out of her mouth in a torrent of unwisely spoken words, 'You think it was easy going into the house of one of the most notorious families in Derbyshire? Especially when Master Hugo deliberately gave me the wrong directions to the Coterels' manor.'

'I beg your pardon?' Robert's placating voice turned to ice.

Sarah swung around from her work and gave Mathilda a warning stare from her shrewd eyes, but Mathilda had had enough. 'He told me to take the wrong road. It was bad enough trying to dodge being seen by that Judas, Geoffrey of Reresby, but honestly! If my Lord Coterel hadn't helped me out, I'd never have got back to Master Hugo's stall. Where, I might add, I made him a fortune selling his trinkets!'

Breathless, regretting her outburst the moment she finished speaking, Mathilda hung her head, muttering, 'I'm sorry, I forgot myself, I ...'

The grip of Robert's hand as it thrust forward and grabbed her chin jarred Mathilda's whole body, 'How dare you speak about one of my most trusted allies like that!'

'I tell you the truth, my Lord!'

'You forget who you are talking to!'

'And you forget that you told me you liked my directness. How can my father possibly raise enough money with two of his children missing? How ...'

Mathilda, her jaw aching from the pressure of Robert's firm fingers, took a ragged breath as realisation dawned. 'You don't intend for them to be able to pay your brothers back, do you? I am too useful to you, and it suits your family to keep mine in debt to them.'

Sarah thumped the jug she held onto the table. 'Foolish girl! You are so sharp you might cut yourself!'

'I can handle this, thank you, Sarah.' Robert dropped Mathilda's chin, gripping her hand instead, 'It seems our guest does not wish to be updated on her position as our ransom, or receive our words of help and advice to get her through this. She apparently knows better.'

'My lord, no, I ...'

Again, Mathilda was cut off mid-sentence, as she saw exactly how unwise she'd been. Coterel had warned her not to reveal Hugo's deception to Robert, and now she wished she'd listened.

A sudden gloating laugh cut through the argument.

Father Richard entered the kitchen demanding a drink from a taciturn Sarah, with an expression that made it plain he was delighted to have witnessed such ire towards Mathilda, before disappearing again as soon as he had what he came for.

Robert shot the view of his retreating brother's back a black look, before rounding on Mathilda, 'Not another word, girl. Not one. Just you listen to me. Master Hugo is a loyal friend. He took no pleasure in informing me that you'd shirked your duties; that you'd made him a loss rather than a profit and had been over two hours late in starting work on his stall. He has nothing to gain from lying to me. Therefore, he did not lie.'

'Of course he did!' Mathilda knew she'd gone too far and was pushing her luck; but it was too late to stop now. 'He's a clever man! It suits him to lie to you. Coterel himself claimed Master Hugo to be untrustworthy, and yet you believe him over me! Me, who has put her life on the line for you in order to save the people I love! You claim to follow the example of Robyn Hode. Well, you're not doing that this time, are you?'

She hadn't cried since she'd been removed from the Folvilles' small cell. Now, as Mathilda found herself back in the tiny stone prison, all her held in grief and fear escaped in a waterfall of distress and frustration. Tears cascaded down her face in torrents, and her cheek stung from the slap of Robert's palm that had met her face with so much power that if she hadn't been sitting down, it would have floored her.

Why hadn't she held her tongue? Her father had told Mathilda many times that her quick retorts would be the death of her. For the first time she considered he might be right. Literally.

Every glimmer of hope she'd had about getting out of this household alive had extinguished. She knew the Coterels were planning to work with the Folvilles, and if the amount of planning they were putting into whatever they intended to undertake was anything to go by, then it would involve a felony of some sort.

To her it seemed as clear as daylight that Master Hugo was jealous of her, but she hadn't a clue why, and she knew her anger at Robert was as much to do with the fact that she wanted him to think better of her than a liar like Hugo. Mathilda cradled her head in her hands. She knew too much- even if she didn't understand any of it- there was no way back from that.

Mathilda wasn't sure how much time had passed since she'd been locked back in the shadows. She hadn't moved from her crouched position on the floor since Robert had left her with the parting words, 'It appears John was right. I was foolish to trust you.'

In spite of the truth of her ill-advised outburst in the kitchen, Mathilda was stung by Robert's words and the expression of disappointment on his face, which was far worse than the anger that it had replaced.

Why is Robert confiding in me one minute and then blasting me with mistrust the next?

The more she thought, the less it made sense.

Thinking back, Mathilda saw how naive she'd been to think she'd be able to leave once she'd delivered that one message. Eustace himself had told her that she was to be their eyes and ears; their messenger. He hadn't said that there would only be one message. She'd been so relieved to have survived her trip to Bakewell that she'd jumped to conclusions.

Weary from her early awakening, Mathilda decided to escape from reality and take solace in sleep. Not bothering to waste time attempting to get comfortable, she rested her head against the mossy stone wall and closed her eyes.

Her doze had been littered with nightmares and faded hopes for the fate of her family, and Mathilda felt a sense of relief when she came back to full consciousness. She blinked. The shadows cast over the four walls loomed over each other as if the slime on the walls was illuminating the space, but then, as her eyes roamed the confided space, she saw a glitter of light just inside the door.

Cautiously reaching out, Mathilda caressed the unmistakeable length of a dagger. The same dagger Robert had lent her the day before.

How had Robert come to find it under her bed where she'd stashed it awaiting a chance to return it to him? Had Sarah or Allward found it and, recognising the colour of the stone to name the weapon as Robert's, returned it to him and forgotten to tell her? And why had he snuck back and left the dagger for her? Had it even been him?

She must have been far more deeply asleep than she'd imagined. Anyone could have opened the heavy wooden door and slid the dagger into her prison. The only fact Mathilda knew for certain was that the weapon hadn't been there before she'd gone to sleep.

~ *Chapter Thirteen* ~

With the scrape of the gaol door opening, Mathilda hastily slid the dagger out of sight up her sleeve. Her heart beat harder as she waited to see who was coming to see her.

Sarah, her jaw set firmer than ever, grey shadows around her eyes suggesting that she hadn't slept too well either, beckoned urgently to Mathilda to follow her.

Bunching her right hand into a fist so that the hidden weapon didn't slide from her sleeve, Mathilda scrambled out of the cell and went with the housekeeper, not to the kitchen as she'd expected, but to a bedroom.

Only when the door had been shut behind them, did Sarah speak. 'This is my Lord Robert's room. You will assist me in making up his bed and collecting his linen for washing. And more importantly, you will keep your mouth shut and listen. We don't have long.'

Hoping that her compliance would lead into Sarah telling her what was going on; she tucked and smoothed the rough sheets as bidden. The hems and backside of her clothes were soiled from the damp and slime of the cell and stuck to her legs as she worked. Mathilda was thankful for the warmth from the dying embers of the fire that had been warming Robert's room during the night.

Moving around the bed, flapping linen into place, Sarah

spoke. 'Listen. All of the brothers are out, but there is no knowing when they'll be back.' The housekeeper moved to the fire and carefully laid a couple of slim twigs onto its embers, ready to coax a stronger flame from the ashes. She sighed heavily. 'Despite the impression my Lord Robert gave you, he knows you did well, Mathilda, but don't let that one success give you the right think it has earned you any favours here. In fact, in truth, your position is now more perilous than it was before.'

Thinking this was something of an understatement considering where she'd just been delivered from, Mathilda asked, 'Please, Sarah, I know I spoke out of turn, and I'm truly sorry for that. But I did exactly what I was ordered to, despite Master Hugo's lies.'

Sensing that Sarah was having a battle with herself as to whether to say more or not, Mathilda added, 'I was left a dagger in the cell. Did you put it there?'

'A dagger?' Sarah's faced grew pale. 'Show me.'

Easing the short-bladed weapon from her sleeve, Mathilda passed it over to the housekeeper, who sat down heavily on the edge of the bed, something Mathilda was sure she'd never normally allow herself to do, especially just after she'd finished making it.

A sense of foreboding shot through Mathilda as Sarah's eyes met hers. 'Something bad has happened, hasn't it?'

Running after Sarah towards the prison, Mathilda's blood pounded in her throat. She didn't know why she was being hurried back into confinement; the housekeeper's worried expression making it plain that this rushed action was for her own safety, not out of malicious intent.

Once Mathilda was back inside, Sarah crouched at the door, glancing behind her nervously, her ears alert from any sound.

'Please, Sarah …'

Shaking her head urgently, Sarah spoke fast, 'Father Richard might return soon, and if he learns I let you out, or indeed have done more than bought you some bread and ale, then he'll have my hide. He's been waiting for an excuse to get me out of here for years.'

'Why?'

'Because his brothers trust me, and he doesn't. The Folvilles haven't always done the right thing, but they believe what they are doing is the best thing. The rector just believes blindly, and his brand of justice is frankly frightening.'

'Why do the others trust you?'

'Because I'm merely their housekeeper, you mean?'

'Forgive me, but yes.'

'I brought them up, raised them from pups. All but for Richard, who was carted off to a monastery at the age of five. He never grew to know or trust me like his brothers did and has always held the fact he was sent away against me, although his departure was none of my doing.' Sarah was getting more agitated, and Mathilda could tell the housekeeper was thinking fast. 'Give me the dagger. It is best we act as though it was never here.'

'What do you mean? Robert obviously thought I might need it.'

'If the dagger wasn't here when you first arrived in the cell, then it wasn't Robert who left it for you. He went back to Derbyshire the moment you were imprisoned.'

Mathilda drew in a sharp breath. 'Do you think he believed me about Master Hugo lying about me after all? Has he gone to quiz the leatherworker?'

'No, he didn't believe you. But I did, and that made Robert think.' Sarah took the dagger and wrapped it in her apron,

'It is very important you do not have this dagger when they come to release you.'

'Why?'

'Word hasn't long come from Derby. Robert didn't get to ask Hugo if he was telling the truth or not.'

'Why not? What word? Who from?'

'From Hugo's apprentice, Roger. Master Hugo was found dead just after Vespers last night. He was stabbed.'

~ *Chapter Fourteen* ~

Mathilda's heart was racing as she thought over everything Sarah had told her before she'd relocked the cell door and rushed back to her kitchen duties. If Mathilda had believed herself to be in a dangerous situation before, that was nothing compared to the position she found herself in now.

The information the leatherworker's lad had imparted to the Folville's stable boy was sparse.

The body of Master Hugo had been found in the wooded ditch that ran to the north side of Twyford, just as the bells for the call to Vespers had rung across the countryside. This meant it had been discovered only a short distance from the workshop belonging to Mathilda's father.

Sarah had kept talking, but there had been no need for her to spell out the peril. Mathilda understood the implications, not to mention the conclusions the sheriff and his bailiff would jump to.

Hugo was a known associate of the Folvilles. Her father, Bertred, not only owed the Folvilles money, but owned the workshop nearest to the place where the body was discovered. On top of that neither she, nor her brother Oswin of Twyford, had been seen around the family home for a few days; this instantly making them suspects.

To make things even worse, someone had left a dagger

in her prison. A dagger that Mathilda was now certain had been placed there to implicate her.

She wondered what Sarah had done with the weapon she'd hurriedly removed from the cell, and what she'd say if questioned by the authorities. Sarah had promised Mathilda that she would not mention she'd been let out of her prison to help with making the beds; but Mathilda knew well that if a heavy-handed method of inquisition was used against the housekeeper, she might not be able to hold to that promise.

It was odd now to recall how hostile Sarah had been to her on arrival in the Folville home only days ago. Forcing herself to drink the broth that Sarah had bought her, Mathilda took comfort from the only piece of welcome news Sarah had given her alongside all the extra worry.

As soon as word of the murder had reached her ears, Sarah had experienced similar fears to Mathilda's and had sent Allward to creep carefully up her family's Twyford home to check on the wellbeing of her father and Matthew.

Although relieved that she'd soon have word of her kin, Mathilda was concerned for the boy. If Allward was spotted spying around Twyford, without being able to give a good reason for being there … she reined in her imagination. There was no point in stewing over things she couldn't control. Wrapping her arms around her crouched legs once again, Mathilda wished that Robert would hurry up and come home so she could talk to him.

For the first time since she'd got to Folville manor, Mathilda was grateful to be locked in a cell so that there was no way she could be believed to be the killer … although someone obviously wanted her to be accused. Otherwise why place the dagger there?

Mathilda heard the shouting even through the thick wooden

door of her captivity. There were at least two male voices and the pleading, placating tones of a woman, who she assumed was Sarah.

Frustrated at not being able to pick out what was being said, Mathilda could tell that slowly the tones were changing from outrage, to the lower pitch of someone doing their best to keep their feelings under control.

After another ten minutes of waiting, the door to her prison swung open. Eustace had a preventative hand on Robert's chest as he attempted to push past his older brother into the cell.

'Mathilda, I would like you to follow me, please.' Eustace gave Robert a warning glare, which clearly declared that although he'd dropped his hand from his chest, he could move it back at any time, possibly with his sword in it.

Following the small group meekly, Matilda found herself in the main hall once more, standing next to Sarah and facing Eustace, Robert, and to Mathilda's dismay, a smug Richard, rector of Teigh, who looked as un-priest-like as ever. If he hadn't been there Mathilda would have spoken unguardedly, however his presence made her wary. He seemed far too delighted by recent events.

'First,' Eustace paid no heed to either of his siblings and addressed the women, 'Allward has returned safely from Twyford.'

Mathilda failed to contain her sigh of relief.

'I see you are pleased.'

'My Lord, I would have hated anything to happen to the boy on my account.'

'Indeed.' Eustace glanced at Sarah, 'you told the girl of Allward's mission?'

The housekeeper bowed in respect, 'When I took her some supper, my Lord. The girl was troubled about her family, and I saw no harm. I apologise if I did wrong.'

Eustace didn't respond to this, addressing Mathilda instead, 'Your father and elder brother are well, although the sheriff's men may well be sniffing around them by the morning. A natural development, as the body of Master Hugo was found so close to your family home and work-shop.' He shot another unreadable expression toward Sarah, 'Our housekeeper has told you of the grisly finding around Vespers.'

'Yes, my Lord.' Mathilda added, 'Thank you for letting me know my family are safe.'

'Safe for now, Mathilda. You know as well as I do that unless something is done the sheriff will want a criminal to go with the crime. I hope he doesn't decide to pick one based on convenience rather than guilt.'

Mathilda opened her mouth to protest at how unfair that would be but closed it again quickly. Such statements were folly.

'Richard and I are going to prepare for our meeting with the Coterels. This separate matter I am leaving to Robert. Making sure the right man is accused is his passion, thanks to his love of stories. I trust his Robyn Hode will bring you both comfort and suggest a few solutions. That is,' Eustace gave his brother a stare, 'if his common sense has kicked in, and he has stopped blaming you.'

Mathilda blanched, forcing herself to keep her eyes on Eustace and not swing around to face Robert. 'Me, my Lord. But I've been in your cell for hours.'

'True. But the rector tells me when he checked on you while you slept, there was a dagger by your feet, and yet when we collected you just now there wasn't. Can you ex-plain that, Mathilda?'

Dread gripped Mathilda. All she could do was repeat

herself. 'I have no dagger, my Lord, and I've been a prisoner since before the hour of Vespers.'

'And yet, Mathilda, why would a man of the church lie to his brother?'

Eustace and a smirking Richard looked at Robert, who in turn, stared at Mathilda with a face as creased with grief and resentment.

The rector gestured a lazy arm towards Sarah. 'Get that woman to search the waif. The dagger was there, and so if it wasn't on the cell floor, it must be about her person.'

Mathilda stiffened, 'My lords, I really don't have …'

Eustace raised a hand to hush her, 'Sarah, if you would please do as my brother requests?'

Tight-lipped, Sarah inclined her head in agreement and went to steer Mathilda towards the curtained bedded area.

'No.' The rector's words were already edged with triumph, 'here, before all of us. I do not trust our housekeeper as much as you do, dear brother.'

'But, sir,' Sarah appealed directly to Eustace, 'I cannot strip the girl before you all.'

The rector however, was adamant. 'I insist. My word has been doubted by a servant. You will do as you're told.'

An imperceptible affirmation toward Sarah from Eustace, and Mathilda found herself turned so that she was facing away from the men sat around the table. Her shawl, surcoat, belt and dress were removed, so that once again she found herself before Robert in only her chemise and undergarments.

As Sarah ran her palms up and down Mathilda's arms, showing the onlookers there nothing was hidden beneath, Richard positively bristled with rage. 'She must have it. Take her shift off!'

'My Lord, I *must* protest!' Sarah's disapproval was

joined by the previously silent Robert.

'Brother that is hardly a decent request for a man of the cloth. I think it is more than clear that there is nowhere on Mathilda's person where a dagger could be secreted. You must have been mistaken.'

'I was not mistaken!' The rector's face burned red in vehemence. 'You are all in this together!' The churchman stormed from the room, his fists clenched, blaspheming in a way that would make even a whore shrink back in horror.

Mathilda tried to think. Why would the rector lie about the dagger? The obvious answer would be that he was the one who'd placed it in her cell ready to be discovered, but why would he do that? His reputation as the most ruthless brother, apart from Eustace, was well deserved if you believed the local rumours of rape and murder, although Mathilda was sure that he'd never been caught or tried for any of his crimes.

Robert's chair scraped against the dirty stone floor as he stood up, his feet still booted for riding, and his cloak grimy from so long in the saddle.

Mathilda studied him properly for the first time that morning. He appeared sallow and strained, but then, he had just lost a friend to murder. She still couldn't understand why Robert was friendly with such an unpleasant man in the first place though. After only one day in his company, Mathilda had no problem with assuming that Master Hugo was capable of upsetting someone enough for them to kill him, but she could see this had rattled Robert more than he would ever be likely to admit.

'Get dressed, Mathilda.' Robert broke off each word as though he was snapping twigs with his voice. 'Sarah, bring the girl to the kitchen. It is time we bought her up to date. Then we have a new mission for her.'

The way he spoke, as if she wasn't even there, sent shivers up Mathilda's spine. This man was a far cry from the Robert who had given her the fine belt she was re-hanging around her waist. She felt his sharp eyes on her, or rather on the belt, as she dressed, her fingers struggling not to fumble over the exquisite fastening.

~ *Chapter Fifteen* ~

The kitchen was welcomingly warm compared to the open space of the hall. Allward was busily sorting out vegetables ready for Sarah to cook up some stew, but when he saw the trio come into the room, he immediately stopped what he was doing, bowed to his master and offered him some ale.

'Thank you,' Robert took the pottery cup. Mathilda immediately recognised it as one of Geoffrey of Reresby's and felt a stab of resentment. The Folvilles were expecting to receive the repayment of her father's ill-advised loan, and yet they hadn't even been bothered to buy his pottery to help him reach that aim.

'Sit down, Mathilda. And you, Allward. We must keep this brief, for there is much to do.'

Mathilda saw that she didn't understand this man at all. Robert may have been only the fourth son of a noble family, but it wasn't usual for someone of his status to sit at the same table as the household servants, and yet he did it freely; although not when his brothers were around. Perhaps his Robyn Hode-inspired principles ran as deeply as he'd proclaimed after all. His changes of mood and actions were harder to keep up with or predict than the weather.

'Allward, explain quickly to Mathilda where you were after the noon bell yesterday.'

The boy shifted uncomfortably, obviously as unused to being treated as an equal as Mathilda was.

'Come on, boy, time is short.'

'Sorry, my Lord.' Allward sat up straight and turned his small round face towards Mathilda. 'Acting on instruction from my Lord Robert, I secretly rode to the household of your father, Bertred of Twyford, to observe their condition.'

Mathilda gasped and turned to Robert, 'My Lord?'

Robert concurred, 'I thought you would be happier if you knew that your family were safe and well. Besides, I owed you an apology, and this seemed a good way to prove that. However, in the light of recent events, my sending of Allward on this mission was timely as well as a gesture of goodwill. You understand the significance of Master Hugo being found so close to your family home, I am sure.'

Mathilda muttered a quiet, 'Yes.'

With a nudge in the ribs from Sarah, Allward carried on his commentary. 'I kept to the outskirts of the workshop and house. I did not wish to be seen.'

'They appeared well?' Mathilda leant towards Allward, as if being closer to him would somehow take her closer to her kin, 'Were they all there? Oswin, as well as my father and Matthew?'

'Your father was in the workshop. If the sounds travelling from the window could be trusted, he was stacking the kiln with fresh pots for firing. He was also talking to someone, but beyond being able to tell you that his companion was male, I know nothing more. I saw no one, and I did not hear him reply. Your brother Matthew could be seen through the kitchen window and from his grumbles about having to do women's work, I suspect he has taken on your duties. I saw no sign of anyone who could have been Oswin; although he may have been the man in the pottery with your father.'

Mathilda was silent for a second and then addressed Robert, 'Thank you, my Lord. I am indeed easier in my mind for knowing that my father hasn't given up hope and is still working to pay his debts.'

'But you wish you knew where Oswin was.'

'I do. May I ask, what time did you leave them, Allward? Before the death of Master Hugo?'

Glancing at Robert to see if he had permission to answer, Allward said, 'At least two hours before, if not more. I'm not good at timekeeping. I saw no sign of the leatherworker or any of his household in the area.'

'And you saw no one else nearby?' Relief gripped Mathilda, as she listened eagerly to the boy's report.

'There was a horse tethered in the orchard, but I assumed that it belonged to whoever was in the workshop with your father, if that wasn't Oswin. I saw no one else around until I got back to the heart of the village, and then it was just locals going about their business. Nor were there any folk about when I returned to Twyford again this evening, after news of Master Hugo's attack had reached us.'

Robert was grave, 'Thank you, Allward, you may get on now. Two such trips in one day will have made you behind with your work.'

Evidently relived to be able to excuse himself, the boy disappeared out of the kitchen.

'You are wondering who was with your father in the workshop around noon?' Robert's thoughtful gaze landed on Mathilda. 'Do you recall if any clients were due to visit him this week?'

'There were none expected when I was last there, my Lord, but of course, that doesn't mean new orders couldn't have come in.' Although, even as she said it, Mathilda knew that to be unlikely. If there had been money coming in soon, she was sure that her father would have pledged it to the Folvilles when he was informed that his daughter had been taken in lieu of repayment of debts, as so Robert would have been aware of it already.

'And you can think of no one it could have been?'

Mathilda shook her head dumbly.

'Then perhaps I should tell you what I think, Mathilda.' Robert banged his cup upon the table. 'I believe that after only a day in your company one of my friends is dead. And this came only hours after he reported to me of how badly you behaved while you worked for him. How you were late to your duties and how you refused to serve one of his most important customers.'

Sarah put a restraining hand on Mathilda's arm as the girl opened her mouth to protest and somehow, she swallowed her words as Robert went on.

'I have sworn to my brothers that you can be trusted, and here I am in an impossible position. Richard is convinced you had a weapon with you in the cell. My dagger, I assume? Where is it now?'

Mathilda gulped. 'It was in my cot. I put it under my mattress when I got back from Bakewell ready to return it to you. When I awoke after falling asleep in the cell, it was by my feet. I swear upon Our Lady herself that I did not have it with me when I went into the dungeon.'

'That does not answer my question, Mathilda. No one knew I had given you the dagger, unless you told them about it.'

'Only Sarah knew, and only because she saw it in the cell when she bought me some broth.'

'This is the truth, my Lord.' Sarah rose from her seat and went to the cutlery store. Checking to make sure no one else was watching, she reached a hand to the very back of the cupboard, and pulled out a rag-covered bundle, which she passed then to Robert.

Unwrapping his dagger, examining it for signs of flesh and blood, of which there were none, he spoke more quietly, 'And you truly did not have this with you when we returned you to the cell?'

'I swear.'

Robert was quiet for a moment, before saying, 'I am grateful to you, Sarah, for stowing this.' He picked up the blade. 'I will return it to its rightful place.'

No one spoke for a while, and Mathilda began to fidget in her seat. She was thinking harder than she ever had before. Who could have put the dagger in the cell? And why? 'May I speak, my Lord?'

'Go on.' Robert positively oozed suspicion, but he held his tongue while she spoke.

'Perhaps whoever put the dagger in the cell wanted to add credence to your belief that I did wrong by Master Hugo. It could suit whoever that person is to paint a black picture of my character.'

'Master Hugo never had cause to lie to me before, Mathilda. I suggest you tread very carefully with what you say next.'

Sweat was gathering on Mathilda's forehead as she ploughed on with her desperate theory, 'Perhaps it was an act meant to add to the suffering of my family. It does seem as if someone is trying to blacken my family's name and reputation. I am here, my father is in debt, and my brother is missing, and now a body has been found near my home.'

'There is another possibility.' Sarah stared meaningfully at Robert while gathering the vegetables prepared by Allward to peel. 'Someone could be out to blacken a name all right, but not Mathilda's.'

Robert stared at the housekeeper, 'Go on.'

'My lord, it was you who proclaimed a trust of Mathilda to your brothers - a trust you have been made to think was broken. I know it was not. Also, it is your friend who has died. A man who, if you will forgive me saying so, was not held in high esteem by many. He was an excellent crafts-man, without doubt, but his personal habits were often questioned. I wonder if it was not Mathilda who was being framed as the target for unpalatable attention, but you, my Lord.'

Mathilda could feel her pulse race as she added, 'Our Lady save us, my Lord! It was your dagger planted in my cell.'

'Tell me, Mathilda, on your soul, and that is not a threat I make lightly, did you tell me the truth? Did Master Hugo send you the wrong way as you claim? Did Coterel help you return to spite Hugo's dishonesty?'

'I promise, my Lord. I promise I have only ever told you the truth.'

~ *Chapter Sixteen* ~

'We have another pressing issue aside from Master Hugo's death. More pressing perhaps.'

The following morning Mathilda found herself standing, once again, across the table from Eustace and Robert in the main hall, but this time without the reassuring presence of the housekeeper, who was catching up with her work. She couldn't begin to imagine what might be more important than clearing her family name of murder. Or at least establishing if it was threatened with that slur in the first place.

The set expression on Eustace's face however told her he was in deadly earnest. Robert and Eustace had been joined by their youngest brother, Walter, whose expression was carefully blank. The tension, which always radiated throughout the hall, felt heightened somehow as Eustace continued, 'The message you collected from Coterel, Mathilda, means that the time for action is almost upon us. In the light of recent events however, it would be foolish for myself or any of my family to be seen in the region intended.'

Deciding not to enquire what that message had meant beyond the obvious arranging of a meeting, Mathilda placed her hands over her belt in an attempt to be calmed by its beauty. For the first time she wished she still had the dagger Robert had loaned her. She had an unpleasant premonition that she was going to need it.

Glancing briefly at his brothers, Eustace continued, 'This means that we require your assistance once more. Mathilda, Robert has assured the three of us that you did act as you claimed during your last visit to Derby after all, and so we are inclined to trust you again.'

The three of us. Did that mean John and Richard did not trust her? Where was the rector anyway? Mathilda wasn't sure if his absence was more or less disturbing than his presence. Aware that she didn't want to find out, Mathilda listened anyway, in the hope that further explanation about her mission would be forthcoming, along with news of her family and any developments in the hunt for Master Hugo's murderer.

For every second of the past twelve hours Mathilda had expected the sheriff's men to come knocking at the Folvilles' front door; but so far there had been nothing. Were the brothers expecting a visit from the authorities as well? Is that why they wanted to be seen to be here, rather than roaming the countryside with messages they shouldn't be relaying?

There was certainly an air of unease that had taken the edge off the family's usual self-assured arrogance.

'At midnight tonight, I was due to meet Coterel myself to speak of future matters. This is no longer possible. You will go in my place, girl, and meet him to present a gesture of my trust and rearrange a new time and place to marshal our plan and make sure of each other's intentions.'

The way Eustace chewed at his words, his fists clenched against the table, made his anger at having to reschedule whatever he'd been plotting obvious.

The blood drained from Mathilda's face as she realised she was going to have to represent the most feared Folville of all. 'Me? How, my Lord?'

Robert took over from Eustace, while all the time the eyes of Walter remained targeted on Mathilda, making her wonder if the man ever blinked. 'There is to be an exchange. A gesture to show that we each understand and agree to this frustrating delay. It will be a show of good faith on both sides. Nicholas Coterel will give us a signal or an item we desire to see and in return, we will give him something. Something you will carry to them for us. It is a system we have used before when legal matters have interfered with our intentions, Coterel will understand what is required without the need for great explanation.'

'But –' her forehead furrowed.

'Mathilda, there has been a murder,' Robert snapped through her sentence, 'The victim can be connected to this household, and at least one member of this household has made no secret of his dislike of Master Hugo.'

'Father Richard, my Lord?' Mathilda whispered the words, uncertain if she was permitted to speak or not; but every instinct in her telling her she was right.

'Indeed.' Robert's brow darkened as he spoke, 'And although Hugo was a loyal friend to me, my Godly brother felt unable to exercise the forgiveness men of the cloth are so often spouting, deciding instead to damn him to hell for his … inclinations. Inclinations he never actually had. Hugo was fiercely loyal and coveted exclusiveness to his friendships, but that was all.'

'Inclinations?' Mathilda searched the faces of the men sat before her. Each one was carefully blank.

Ignoring her enquiry, Robert continued, 'you will be escorted on your journey, but from the shadows. To all intents and purposes, you will appear to be alone.'

There was a silence, and Mathilda took her chance, 'The

item I am to deliver?'

'It is a package. Only small. You'll easily be able to conceal it about your person.'

As nothing was to be achieved by arguing, Mathilda decided to be practical. 'But surely I am to be accompanied by someone else as well as my hidden escort? A woman out on her own so late at night will cause suspicion.'

'It will be me alone.' Robert walked towards the fire to warm his hands, 'I will be keeping to the trees. You won't see me, but I will be there at all times. The route you will take is wooded on either side. My concealment will not be difficult.'

'And what of the concealment of others? Outlaws are not unknown between here and Bakewell. I could be taken by them or by the sheriff's men if they identify me as my father's daughter. They are bound to suspect him of having a hand in Master Hugo's death.'

Robert bristled. 'I have given my word that you'll be kept safe. That should be enough for you.'

Mathilda said nothing else, hoping that his surveillance would be enough to keep her safe. Wishing Robert would stop believing all the poison fed to him by Master Hugo prior to his death, she couldn't help thinking that she'd be safer if Eustace was shadowing her.

'May I ask what I might expect to transport back in return?'

'I will tell you as we travel to the meeting place, which isn't as far as Bakewell.' Robert nodded to his brothers for confirmation, inviting them to add anything he may have omitted from the instructions.

Addressing Mathilda, Eustace said, 'just be careful, girl. It isn't only your safety wrapped up in this mission. Your family owes me. Money, it is becoming increasingly clear, as each day goes by, isn't something they can easily repay. Your services are becoming a more permanent form of payment by the day. If harm comes to you, and you are no longer able to provide those services, then I will extract another form of payment from your father. I am sure that is not something you want.'

'No, my Lord.' Mathilda stared at her feet. The threatening tone of Eustace's voice was replaced by Robert talking again, but she hadn't heard what was being said. She was too busy attempting to marshal her thoughts and get a grip on the thought that was beginning to nag in the back of her mind, to listen.

Allward had reported that her father had been in the workshop talking with someone before Hugo's death. So, who was the visitor? A new customer? It had to have been. Their regular customers had all but disappeared thanks to Geoffrey of Reresby and his fellow importers.

And where was Oswin? Was he out trying to acquire more money to pay off the debt quicker? There weren't many ways to earn enough extra income that were worth leaving the family business for, and none she could think of were legal. Mathilda's blood chilled as she considered some of the risks Oswin could be taking to help the family. If he was still alive? She closed her eyes. There were some things she didn't want to consider.

Oswin might have been two years older than her, but Mathilda had always looked after him. A large, gentle soul, Oswin always did what he was told; without necessarily spending a lot of time thinking about the consequences.

'Mathilda?'

Aware of a pair of startling blue eyes staring into hers, Mathilda came back to earth, shocked to find she was still in the hall, with everyone was staring at her.

Robert placed one of his large hands on her shoulder, 'Did you understand that? Do you know what you are to do?'

'I have to save my family.' She spoke more to herself than to the Folville before her. Then, forgetting her servile status, she stared back at Robert, pushing her shoulders back as she addressed him, 'and if that means I have to stay here and spy or send messages for you and then so be it; although the logic in keeping me here when I could be at home helping them earn money to get you what you are due escapes me, my Lord.' She paused and placed her hands on her hips. They needed her, so for now at least she could risk a little impertinence. 'But please could you tell me exactly how indebted my father is? If I know how much we owe, then perhaps I can help them reach the goal.'

Robert gestured to his seated brothers as if asking how much he should say.

Eustace, with a confirming nod from the ever-mute Walter, said 'The debt your father owes is only partly financial. We have been informed by a reliable source that he did some further damage that needs paying for. Damage that money will not make that better. Only his inconvenience will do. His punishment is to find the money he owes without your help. Without his right hand. Since the death of your mother, Mathilda, you are that right hand.'

Thinking furiously, trying to remember a time in which her father had defamed or inconvenienced her captors, Mathilda was about to ask the nature of this inconvenience, when Eustace and Walter rose to their feet, 'Robert, the girl knows enough. Too much for her own safety, perhaps. Any more would be unwise for us and dangerous for her. I suggest you repeat the instructions, she plainly didn't hear them. Then hand her over to Sarah. She can make herself useful and work in the kitchen until it is time to leave.'

Suddenly, as one, the brothers swept around the table and stood before Mathilda like a solid wall of intimidation.

Eustace, grabbing her chin with one hand, the other resting on the hilt of his sword, spoke with a final deliberation. 'Some advice, young woman; don't ask any more questions. Do what you are told, and perhaps one day you'll get to go home.'

~ *Chapter Seventeen* ~

Mathilda was kneading the dough for the day's bread so roughly that Sarah was beginning to think it would only be fit for the pigs. 'Have you never made bread before?'

Stopping the pumping movement of her elbows, Mathilda kept up the movement of her hands in the mixture. 'I was thinking about tonight.' Continuing to work at a far more sedate place, lightening her touch so she aerated the dough properly, Mathilda was aware that the housekeeper was watching her. 'Do you know what they want me to do, Sarah?'

'Yes.'

'Oh.' Mathilda didn't know what else to say. The tone of Sarah's single word response had felt final and was obviously not going to be elaborated on.

Knocking the bread dough into shape before leaving it to rest, Mathilda reached into a pail of clean water Allward had provided and washed the flour from her hands. All the time she scrubbed at her skin, Mathilda considered the instructions Robert had given her. They seemed straightforward. Too straightforward.

The meeting with the Coterels was to be at midnight that night. As the sun began to go down, she and Robert would ride to a mid-point between Ashby Folville and Derby.

When they were about a mile from the meeting place, they would split up, and she would continue alone until she met one of the Coterels. Probably Nicholas.

Keeping a sensible distance away from her would be Robert. He'd assured her this shadowing was merely to avoid any unwanted questioning should the sheriff's men be lurking in the area after Hugo's death. Mathilda had to concede that, although she didn't want to go alone, even just for that last mile, this was sensible.

Once she'd located the Coterels, Mathilda wouldn't have to say anything. All that was asked of her would be the handing over of the package Robert would entrust to her when they were ready to go. Then an item would be given to her in return, and she would proceed back along the path she'd come from, before Robert returned her to the safety of the Folville manor.

Pointing to a pile of apples that needed peeling, Sarah nodded with satisfaction as Mathilda set to work without complaint. 'I hope you don't mind that I persuaded Robert to let you help me today. I told him that providing I keep an eye on you, you are of more use around the house than trapped in a cell.'

Not knowing what else to say, Mathilda said, 'Thank you, Sarah.'

'A gentle prod to recall that now, more than ever, it is vital to give the community the impression that Robert is interested in you as a future wife was needed. He can hardly do that if you are closeted in a cell. You helping with domestic chores will support the falsehood.'

With all that had happened in the last forty-eight hours, Mathilda had forgotten about the front she and Robert were supposed to be presenting to the world. She was about to ask why it was it was even more important now, but Sarah changed the subject.

'I see you must have been a good housekeeper for your family, when you're not being distracted.'

Mathilda looked up from her work. 'Thank you, Sarah. I hope I was. My mother was very efficient; I try to be like her.'

Moving to the door to check they wouldn't be overheard, Sarah worked at Mathilda's side. 'Don't react, just in case we are watched. I'm about to tell you something that I don't think the brothers know yet.'

With a prickle of perspiration dotting the back of her neck, Mathilda exhaled softly, 'what is it Sarah?'

'I was concerned for your safety in tonight's mission. It seemed too easy somehow. Too arranged. So I sent the stable boy to review another location yesterday.'

Mathilda's knife slipped, nicking her finger, causing her to drop the fruit. Sucking at the tiny cut, she breathed out her enquiry, 'Is there news of Oswin?'

'I believe so. The lad rode to the Coterel manor. He entered the stable block and asked for directions he didn't really require so he could poke around. He spied a young man answering to your brother's description working as a servant in the Coterel household.'

'Oswin is with the Coterels! Are you sure?'

'No, Mathilda, I'm not sure, but it is likely.'

Mathilda suddenly remembered the feeling of being watched she'd had when she was talking to Nicholas Coterel. It had been merely a sensation of being observed, not the sinister feeling that being observed by a stranger can give you. Had those eyes belonged to Oswin?

'And you don't think Robert and the other Folvilles know about this?'

'As I said, I don't know for certain. If they do, then I

can't think why they haven't told you.'

Mathilda suspected they probably did know, and it was likely that they hadn't told her because it suited them to keep her worried about her brother. If she had more than one family member to be concerned for it would make doubly sure of her obedience.

Keeping this theory to herself, Mathilda said, 'Sarah, please don't think me ungrateful, but why are you helping me like this? It's such a risk for you and Allward, not to mention the stable lad.'

Sarah's usual austere countenance broke into a hitherto unseen gentle concern. 'I told you that I raised almost all the brothers,' she peered around her, alert and wary even in her softer state, 'and I know it's wrong to have a favourite, but I do.'

'Robert?'

Her tone full of regret, Sarah said, 'I have tried to keep him safe. Tried to look after him and his family, but they walk into trouble, those men.'

'Their intentions are good.'

Sarah's expression reverted to its usual shrewd state. 'Do you truly believe that, Mathilda?'

'I didn't at first. But now, I think we can assume that the sheriff's men will be sniffing around my family; and knowing full well how the sheriff likes to find a perpetrator for the crimes in his jurisdiction, even if it isn't the right one – well, some justice is better than none.'

'Have you heard of Folville's Law, Mathilda?'

'No.'

'What you're doing here, that's Folville's Law. The meeting tonight, that's Folville's Law as well. Just as, if my suspicions are correct, the killer of Master Hugo will be found using Folville's Law.'

'You mean this family takes the law into their own hands and administers its own justice. A more direct form of justice.'

'I mean exactly that.'

'Like in the Robyn Hode stories.'

Sarah smiled. 'You've heard the travelling players sing of Robyn Hode?'

'Yes, at the fair last year. I'd heard a few before then as well though. My mother used to sing them to me.'

'You remember them well?'

'I've always had a good memory for words.'

'Is that so?' The housekeeper picked up some firewood and gestured to Mathilda to follow suit.

Moving into the deserted hall, Sarah knelt to the grate and tapped the floor for Mathilda to sit with her. 'My grandfather taught me many such songs. Not the Hode ones, of course, they're too modern; but the lines he sang with his fellow soldiers after the failure of De Montfort's revolt were similar in sentiment.'

Mathilda gasped; even now, over six decades since Simon de Montfort and his barons had failed in their rebellion against the excesses of King Henry III, it wasn't sensible to mention any sympathies towards them. Mathilda felt oddly flattered that the initially hostile housekeeper was confiding in her in such a way.

'There's one verse that has stayed with me. It's from a song I used to sing to the Folville boys when they were children. Sometimes I wonder if that was such a wise thing to do when they were so impressionable, still …'

Then, much to the younger woman's surprise, Sarah began to sing.

'Right and wrong march nearly on equal footing;

there is now scarcely one who is ashamed of doing what is unlawful;
the man is held dear who knows how to flatter;
and he enjoys a singular privilege ....'

There was a moment's quiet before Mathilda said, 'Things haven't changed much, have they?'

'Sadly, child, they have. It's worse now, much worse.' With a final placing of the cut wood on the fire, Sarah added, 'I think it's time to answer the question you haven't asked me.'

'Which one? I have a great many questions.'

Sarah grinned, 'I am referring to the question that is most important in the light of Master Hugo's death. Why it is you need to be seen to be Robert's companion at this time, more than ever?'

'What do you mean?'

'There has been gossip, in its most cruel form. I am sorry, Mathilda, but it is best you know. This cruel rumour places my Lord Robert as the object of Master Hugo's unholy affection.'

'Are you ready?'

Robert, dressed from head to toe in brown and grey to aid his concealment in the woods, reined in his horse as the same bleary-eyed stable lad who'd possibly located Oswin hoisted Mathilda into her saddle.

'I am.' Mathilda didn't feel at all ready, but with a new resolve engendered by Sarah's confidences and the knowledge that Oswin was very probably alive, even if he wasn't free to go home, she sat with all the confidence of a woman who fully expected to be Robert's future wife. A concept she was surprised to find didn't repulse her as she'd assumed it would; especially now she knew precisely why it was so vital to her survival, her father's success in paying off his debt and Robert de Folville's very life.

~ *Chapter Eighteen* ~

Robert said nothing as they rode through the subdued evening light; his concentration taken up entirely by his surveillance of the landscape around them.

For once the quiet didn't make Mathilda uncomfortable. She welcomed more time to think back over the conversation she'd had with the housekeeper that afternoon.

Sarah had confided in her while they'd made up the hall fire, then had gone on to discuss more about the troubles in London. She'd told Mathilda that a merchant had been adding to the buzz of tattle that had been circulating at the weekly market for some months now. Unwisely telling anyone who'd listen, rather too loudly, about the latest liberties taken by King Edward II's widow Isabella. She, and her lover Mortimer, had stolen power from the Crown almost two years ago, and violence and corruption had become commonplace in London as a result. That unrest was spreading fast in every direction across England as the population remained unsure who was actually in charge.

The conversations that Mathilda's father and brothers had about the way the country was being run, when they knew they were out of earshot of anyone who might report them, had given her the impression that the sheriff, Sir Robert Ingram, and his bailiff were already corrupt and that there were few things they'd refrain from doing if the money was right.

While Sarah had been talking to her about events in the south, the thoughts that had been vying for attention in Mathilda's head had begun to crystallise. The fog of fear for her own safety had lifted, and she was beginning to see the reality of the circumstances more clearly.

Although undeniably tough and uncompromising, the Folvilles, and quite probably the Coterels as well, had decided that the law was failing them. That was why they did what they did. They weren't the good guys, and Mathilda certainly disapproved of many of their more extreme actions, but compared to the avaricious excesses of the authorities, they were the lesser of two evils. In Mathilda's eyes they became more like Robyn Hode and his outlaws every day. After all, Hode's Merry Men were far from saints, but compared to those who held the power within their stories, they were principled indeed.

Breaking the tension as they left Ashby Folville far behind them, Robert pointed the horses towards a path that would take them deep into Charnwood Forest. 'Are you scared of the dark, Mathilda?'

'No.' Mathilda spoke honestly. 'But I am afraid of what may lurk in the dark.'

'Very wise.' Robert smiled, reminding Mathilda of how handsome he could look. 'In just over ten miles the path will split into two. I will go one way and you the other. For a few paces you will be alone, but after that the path sweeps around, and I will be riding parallel to you again, albeit with a narrow dividing wall of tress.'

Not allowing her hands to tremble with the nerves that had been bubbling in her stomach, Mathilda pushed her shoulders further back and sat bolt upright in the saddle.

'And the package?'

'You already have it.'

'No, my Lord, I don't.' Mathilda's voice gave away her uncertainty. Had Sarah been meant to give her something before they left the manor?

'I'm afraid you do.' Robert reined his horse in next to Mathilda's, bringing them to a halt.

Reaching out a hand, he gently flipped Mathilda's cloak to one side to reveal the finery of her leather girdle belt. He smoothed it with a single finger of his gloved hand. 'That is their prize, Mathilda.'

'My belt?'

'Sadly, yes.'

'But …'

Robert nodded, 'I regret I told you it was for you. It was my honest intension for you to keep it. However, with the death of Hugo …' He lapsed into a silence that spread out like splayed fingers into the grey night as the tress thickened around them.

The horses moved forward again. Mathilda shivered as Robert spoke in a more guarded fashion, 'The belt is to be used as proof of our goodwill to Coterel. It is a valuable object, and now Hugo has gone, it is worth a great deal more.'

Nodding with sad understanding, Mathilda stroked one hand over the intricate lattice work, 'I shall miss it. I've never owned an object of such beauty before, even if only for a little while.'

'I almost did, briefly, but I fear I may have ruined my chances.'

Mathilda turned sharply toward Robert. 'My Lord?'

Saying no more on the subject, Folville pointed instead to a fork in the path. They were getting close to their undisclosed destination.

The texture of the air changed the second Robert was out of sight. Despite her resolve to be brave and see this through to the end, Mathilda was frightened. Spurred on by the hope that if Nicholas Coterel was in receptive mood, she would take the chance to ask him about Oswin, Mathilda felt aware of every breath she took, as though her body was savouring the sensation while she could still do it.

The trees felt as if they were closing in on either side of her and that the light of the moon was being physically snuffed out by the close-knit overhanging branches. With each step of the horses, all the jolly outlaw stories Mathilda had ever heard the mummers sing and had watched being acted out in fairs and markets took on a sinister edge. Forgotten were all the verses about getting the better of a corrupt authority. All she could recall from them now, were the verses of violence. How the outlaws had skulked in the forest, how they had waylaid travellers and demanded a tax to pass by.

The words '*To invite a man to dinner, and then him to beat and bind. It is our manner,*' drowned out the lull of the line she usually recalled: '*For he was a good outlaw, and did poor men much good ...*'

Her ears alert for every rustle of leaves and every possible crack of a twig under foot or hoof, Mathilda battled her muddled thoughts, entwining them into the ballads she held so dear. From the depths of her mind she remembered the devious potter who'd double-crossed Robin. '*... The potter, with a coward's stroke, smot the shield out of Robin's hand...*'

'The potter!' Mathilda mumbled the words rather than spoke them. The gloom surrounding her became more suffocating, and her eyes flitted from one side of the path to the other as another line of verse formed on her soundless lips.

'I have spied the false felon, as he stands at mass ...'

She wasn't sure why the random utterance of this line from Robyn Hode and the Monk made all the hairs on the back of her neck stand up, but with a feeling that a ghost had crossed her path, Mathilda tried even harder to spot the shadow of Robert through the trees. Although she knew that being unable to see him didn't mean he wasn't there, she wished she could glimpse him every few paces or so.

Feeling cold and alone, Mathilda's common sense refused to unlatch itself from her overactive imagination. Her thoughts flew to Master Hugo and the terror he must have experienced as he realised what was happening to him. As the dagger got closer and closer ...

A shadow fell across the ever-narrowing path, and Mathilda startled as her horse snorted into the stagnant air. Pulling the reins sharply, she came to a stop and looked behind her.

Mathilda was convinced she was being watched, and not just by Robert.

Was it Robert, a Coterel, soldiers, men out on the hue and cry, or outlaws observing her? Mathilda pressed on again, her unease making her grip her leather reins so tightly that they were in danger of cutting her palms.

Despite her fear about what she might find around the next turn of the thinning path, the image of Hugo wracked with pain continued to take prime position in Mathilda's consciousness – a vision which abruptly contorted into the mocking face of Richard Folville, the rector of Teigh ...

A voice came out of the night, its hollow echo bouncing off the trunks of the closely packed trees. Mathilda tugged her palfrey to an abrupt halt, straining her eyes and ears to every possible sight and sound. The words she'd heard could have come from any direction, and although she felt the presence of another person - no, other people - there was more than one set of eyes trained on her, she was sure of that, Mathilda couldn't work out where they were concealed. Would they appear in front of her, or would they creep up from behind?

Hoping Robert was as close as he'd promised to be, the voice came again, less muffled this time. 'Mathilda of Twyford?'

It was more of a question than a statement and hoping that the fact they knew her name meant that they were expecting her and must therefore be the Coterels and not the sheriff's men, she summoned up her courage.

'I am Mathilda of Twyford.'

There was a faint rustle of leaves to her right, and the stately figure of Nicholas Coterel came striding through the trees. Mathilda was surprised he was on foot and immediately supposed that the other person she'd sensed in the area was probably a groom, with his master's stallion held at a safe distance.

'I'm pleased to see you well, Mistress Twyford. I feared Master Hugo might mistreat you after our prank at his expense.'

Having taken comfort in the reassurance from Robert that she wouldn't have to say anything during the exchange, Mathilda found herself unprepared for pleasantries and gabbled, 'Thank you, my Lord, I am well.'

'Good. Not that it matters now that leech has been hurried to hell. Tell me, was the belt maker disquieted by your prompt return to the market after our last encounter?'

Mathilda felt a surge of hope in her chest. If Coterel was saying Hugo had double-crossed her, then maybe Robert would finally believe the truth of it. 'He was my Lord, thank you for helping me return to him as I'd promised.'

'You are welcome. So, to business.' Nicholas gestured towards the girdle Mathilda wore around her waist, before calling out, 'Robert, you may as well come forth. We have scoured the area. A hue and cry has not been mustered to hunt Hugo's killer this deep into Charnwood tonight, and there isn't a soldier for miles.'

Robert stepped from the cloaking trees. He was without his horse as well. Dipping his head to his Derbyshire neighbour, Robert held out a hand, helping Mathilda from her mount so she could remove the girdle.

Keeping her face as neutral as possible, not wanting either of the men to see how much she disliked handing over the belt, Mathilda wordlessly passed it to Nicholas.

Holding it up to what moonlight there was, Nicholas closed his eyes and ran the tips of his fingers over the lattice pattern. 'I believe I was informed correctly.' Then, calling into the trees behind him he said, 'Tell me, Oswin, what do you think?'

Mathilda's heart soared as her youngest brother strode into the small clearing. His face was its usual circle of good-naturedness as she ran into his outstretched arms.

'If I could have your attention, Master Twyford!' Coterel clipped his words, and Oswin, his face a shock of embarrassed red, came to his lord's side.

'Is this as we suspected?'

Oswin's chunky fingers stroked the carved leather as if it was of the finest ceramics. 'No question, my Lord.'

Coterel's brow creased. 'You're sure. No mistake?'

'Positive, my Lord.' Oswin went to give the girdle back to Nicholas, but Coterel waved it back in Mathilda's direction.

'Never let it be said that I deprived the beautiful woman of an ally of her finery.'

Robert's face darkened, but he made no comment on the subject as a stunned Mathilda clipped the belt back in place, an enquiry bursting from her lips like a demand. 'I was under the impression that you wanted the finery as a token of trust, my Lord. Why did you wish to see the belt up close only to refuse to take it? '

'I will tell you on one condition.'

'Only one?' Robert's sarcasm was as thick as honey, but Coterel ignored him.

'I will share what we suspect in this matter if you will agree to assist in the matter we were going to discuss before that damn leatherworker got up enough people's noses to get himself murdered and delay our cleansing of the corruption in this area.'

It was clear from Robert's expression how difficult he was finding it to not to mention how much the corrupt nature of the legal system often worked to their benefit, 'My brothers and I are in agreement. Our families will act together on that matter. Eustace suggests a gap of three to six months for planning and to let the dust settle on Hugo's death.'

'Four months. At most.'

Robert paused before saying, 'Agreed.'

Obviously satisfied with whatever agreement had been made, Nicholas then addressed Oswin. 'You may return to Ashby Folville with your sister as discussed and share our thoughts about the murder with her current household. However, if you do not return to me by dusk the day after tomorrow, there will be consequences. Yes?'

'Yes, my Lord.' Oswin bowed.

Mathilda turned to Robert, her face full of wonder. 'Oswin is the item we are to collect?'

'You made it plain that your brothers are as important to

you as mine are to me.'

Speechless, unable to keep up with Robert's changeable nature where she was concerned, Mathilda turned her attention back to the two men who'd travelled from the Peak District.

Giving his sister a look which told her plainly to ask no questions for the time being, Oswin took Mathilda's bridle and made ready to lead her palfrey back along the forest path.

'You may tell them everything once you are in the safety of the Folville manor, Oswin.' Then disappearing into the forest, Nicholas called over his shoulder 'I'd make that girl yours fast, Robert, before I'm tempted to steal her from you.'

~ *Chapter Nineteen* ~

Mathilda's head buzzed like a hive of bewildered bees.

Her need to ask Oswin why he was working with the Coterels was losing out to her desire to ask Robert precisely what his intentions towards her were. On the other hand, she was desperate to find out more about the significance of Oswin and Nicholas's examination of her girdle, not wanting to sort through her mounting suspicions about the leatherworker's murder.

Mathilda was convinced the dagger had been placed in her cell by the rector, and the more she thought about it, the more convinced Mathilda was that the holy Folville must be mixed up in Hugo's death. Yet it still felt ridiculous to think Richard would kill Master Hugo. For a start, he was a cleric, albeit one with a history of violence. But an attack on Hugo was an attack on Robert, and why would he want to hurt his brother in that way?

Mathilda had a feeling Robert would scoff at her ideas and probably be furious with her for even having them in the first place. She didn't want to upset him after his recent act of extreme kindness in ensuring Oswin was returned to her, if only briefly. And yet she was unable to shift the notion that the rector had something to hide.

As they'd travelled the weary miles back, Oswin had

said nothing, but every so often he'd give his sister the familiar comforting smile he used whenever he was telling her everything was going to be all right. It wasn't until he helped her dismount, tired and dusty from the road and the earliness of the daylight hour, that Mathilda finally took her chance.

Speaking under her breath, not sure if Oswin would want to share his answer publicly, she said, 'Why are you working for the Coterels?'

Dealing with the removal of her palfrey's saddle without looking at his sister, Oswin murmured softly into his chores, 'Rumour is rife that the Folvilles and Coterels are planning something together. Something big. My sister was kidnapped by the Folvilles; so where else would I go to learn about her safety than to their main rivals and now, it would seem their confederates? I wanted to make sure you couldn't be implicated in whatever they are planning. When they heard I was your kin, they didn't hesitate to appoint me.'

Impressed by this unusually sharp thinking by her brother, Mathilda had no time to ask further of him. Robert was ushering them towards a plainly impatient Eustace and a taciturn Walter.

Consoling herself with the fact that Oswin had gone to the Coterel manor of his own free will and had not been forced into service as she had, Mathilda followed her new employers – or kidnappers, or owners? She wasn't sure who they were to her, or who she was them any more beyond a bargaining counter; a fact, Mathilda realised, that made her no different from most women born into the families of the gentry.

'Off to bed with you, Mathilda.'

In her humiliated embarrassment she forgot her manners, squarely facing Eustace. 'But I went all that way in the dark and –'

'And now we don't need you. You did a good job, but you must be tired. You will be allowed to see your brother before he returns to Bakewell. You were up all night walking the paths of Charnwood Forest, Mathilda. Sleep now, while you can.'

Without Sarah to back her up, Mathilda felt fatigue grip her, making her as tired as Eustace had suggested she was. Rather than wasting energy protesting, she went directly to her cot hidden away in the corner of the hall. Privately, however, she vowed to stay awake as long as she could to listen to the family's conversation.

Mathilda wrapped herself in her blanket to wait, alert for any sign of trouble, from either inside or outside the hall. It was of increasing concern to her that not one soldier had come calling, and that the hue and cry hadn't been out hunting for Hugo's killer. Why not? Had someone stopped them from tracking the murderer down?

Lying unmoving, so as not betray that she was eavesdropping, Mathilda continued to speculate about the lack of effort being taken by the law towards finding Hugo's murderer. It was so foreign to the usual pattern. The sheriff was generally overzealous in his keenness to wrap up a case and get the 'guilty' party parcelled for judgement before the day of the crime was over. The fact that she had neither seen nor heard a soldier or a man asking questions made Mathilda wonder if any measures had been taken by the law at all. And if it hadn't, then why not?

There was a scrape of chairs, so Mathilda knew that at least some of the men had sat down; then at last, the sound of Eustace's voice travelled across the hall.

'Master Twyford, Robert tells me that you were the offering of surety from Nicholas Coterel, and that you have leave to stay with your sister until early tomorrow, when you must return.'

'Yes, my Lord.' She could imagine Oswin giving a bow, his large frame making rather clumsy work of the respectful gesture.

'And I am given to believe by Robert that, in an unprecedented gesture of compassion, Coterel didn't take the girdle belt from Mathilda, but merely examined it. Can you explain to me why this was, Master Twyford, or am I to assume that Nicholas has merely taken a liking to your sister?'

Mathilda could feel an embarrassed glow fill her up as, from her spy hole through the curtains; she caught the flicker of displeasure that this suggestion sent over Robert's face.

'My Lord Coterel felt it was enough that the gesture of the gift was made. He had no intension of doing more than examine it. Naturally he is more preoccupied with the nature of your forthcoming plan.'

Eustace grunted. 'And so he should be. This business with Hugo is poorly timed. Still, at least he is keen to carry on. Four months did he say, Robert?'

Inclining his head, Robert said, 'De Vere, La Zouche, and De Heredwyk will all be agreeable to the change in date.'

'As long as it happens!' Eustace banged a fist upon the table, 'Never did I think this land would be at the mercy of a justice worse than Belers, yet this …'

'Brother!' Robert shouted the warning, gesturing to both Oswin and Mathilda, 'we agreed to keep his name quiet, did we not, to protect those who do not need to know?' Turning his attention back to Oswin, Robert said, 'The Lord Coterel gave you leave to tell me why he was keen to see the belt Mathilda wears. Will you please do so?'

The belt again? Mathilda leaned further forward and pressed her ear as close to the dividing tapestry hanging as she could.

'My Lord, on market day, one of the kitchen staff was instructed to purchase a new pitcher for the kitchens. When the girl served ale from it to my Lord Nicholas, he recognised the similarity of the pattern on it to one he'd seen before. To the design he had noticed on the girdle that surrounds my sister's waist.'

Mathilda sucked in a low breath. Of course! She knew she'd seen the pattern before but hadn't been able to recall where. It was on the pitcher being carried so carefully by the girl she'd seen walking away from the market when she'd been hunting for the Coterel manor.

Obviously bored with the conversation now he'd heard Coterel's response to his message, Eustace barked, 'I fail to see why this concerns us.'

Robert held up his hand. 'Go on, Oswin. What do you and Coterel suspect?'

'It occurred to my master that if Geoffrey of Reresby suspected that Master Hugo had been stealing his signature pattern, it made sense that he should have been hovering around Master Hugo's stall to examine the leather ware for himself. It also gives him a motive for attacking Master Hugo.'

The men were talking again, but Mathilda was unable to hear them properly. Pulling her blanket tighter around her shoulders, she tugged off her boots, her heart thumping so loud that she thought it would be heard and give her away. Creeping to the edge of the tapestry divider on her stocking feet, hoping her shadow wouldn't cast across the hall and give her away, Mathilda could see the outline of Eustace's back through the frayed needlework as he addressed Oswin,

'You have other news on this matter?'

'I do, my Lord. The pottery merchant Reresby has long been a plague on my family. He has been undercutting my father's prices for some time.'

Eustace had run out of patience and, swooping around the table, he picked Oswin up by the neck and rammed him back against the nearest stone pillar. 'We agreed you would be returned to Coterel. We didn't say in how many pieces. Now spit out whatever it is you are finding so difficult to trip off your tongue!'

Forcing herself not run to her brother's side, Mathilda watched as Robert unpeeled Eustace's hand from Oswin's throat. 'He can't tell us anything if you have your hand at his throat.'

The glare Eustace gave his brother would have quelled a lesser man, but Robert held his stare. 'We need to hear him speak!'

With a sharp nod of encouragement from Robert, Oswin went on, 'After Mathilda came to work for you, I ran. I knew the only way to find out what had happened to her while in your care was to disappear and grab information where I could. When I heard rumour of your future plans to work with the Coterels, I decided to get employment with them.'

'They took you just like that?

'No, my Lord, they took me because I told them the truth. It pays them to know what you are up to as much as it pays you to know as much as you can about them.'

Walter snorted. 'Well said. And ...'

'I saw Mathilda come to the manor to report to my Lord Nicholas before she went to help at the Bakewell market. My Lord did not trust Master Hugo and bid me follow my sister on the return to the market in case he treated her badly. He feared that Hugo would hold a grudge of jealousy against her for being held in my Lord Robert's affection.'

Walter snorted louder than before, reminding Mathilda of a disgruntled pig.

Ignoring his younger brother's derision, Robert pulled out a chair and bid their visitor sit down, 'what did you see or hear, Oswin? Don't miss out anything. Anything!'

'Are you sure, my Lord?' Oswin spoke directly to Robert, whose face furrowed as he looked from Eustace to Walter and back again.

Speaking frustratingly quietly, forcing Mathilda to risk taking another few steps from the curtains so she could hear, hoping that the men would be far too concentrated on each other and their conversation to turn around. 'I know what is said behind cupped hands about Hugo and I, Master Twyford. As do my brothers. However, I would keep it from your sister if I am able, so please keep your voice down in case she is not yet asleep.'

Mathilda took one noiseless step backwards, touched that he cared enough to want to shield her from the hearsay that surrounded him and glad that she hadn't told him Sarah had already confided to her what vile words were said about Robert and his fallen friend.

Oswin still appeared uncomfortable, but he kept going, addressing Eustace directly, 'May I ask, my Lord, which of your brothers decided that my father should pay for his slander with the kidnap of his only daughter? Was it the same brother who suggested to my father that your family could lend him some money to help his business recover from the damage Geoffrey of Reresby has done in the first place?'

Robert froze to the spot, while Walter and Eustace stared at each other.

After what felt like an eternity, Robert finally asked Eustace, 'Was it his idea?'

Mathilda didn't need to hear Eustace's reply. Although no name had been accused, suddenly all the pieces fell into place.

The dagger appearing in her cell while she'd slept. The rumours about Robert that Sarah had shared with her. The finding of Hugo's body so close to her father's home. All of it. Everything was beginning to make sense – except for the lack of sheriff's men hammering on the door asking questions.

'Was it him?' Robert spat the word this time.

As the tension in the hall trebled Mathilda knew she had to act now; tell the brothers right away what she suspected. If she didn't, she had the feeling that there would be another murder very much closer to home.

~ *Chapter Twenty* ~

'Mathilda! How dare you? I told you to –'

'My Lord, please!' Mathilda beseeched Robert at top speed, 'Forgive my interruption. I was listening, and I know I wasn't supposed to be, but you must have known I would. And I must speak. It is very important. I think I know what this is all about.'

Eustace pulled out a chair and thumped down onto it. 'For St George's sake, Robert! If she is to be your woman you're going to have to learn to control her. We no longer have to tolerate her constant questions, because I've damn well worked it out myself.' The second Folville brother crashed his palm down upon the table in frustration. 'Damn the man's hide! He'll be the death of all of us!'

Swinging around to Walter, who was already standing, his hand on the hilt of his sword, Eustace barked the instruction that Mathilda had already anticipated he'd make. 'Ride to Leicester. John, Thomas, and Laurence should all be there. Tell them we need a family meeting here. Now.'

Mathilda yelled in warning. 'You can't just … it isn't what you think …' But her words were lost to the rapid flurry of activity.

Eustace had already left the hall. Mathilda could hear him shouting at Allward to find Sarah and bring her to the kitchen. Walter had vanished, presumably to grab whichever horse was the quickest to saddle, leaving Oswin standing looking from his sister to Robert de Folville and back again, his expression a picture of confusion. Sarah hurried past to the heart of her domestic domain, proved that Eustace's shouting had yielded results.

In the middle of this breakout of chaos Robert took Mathilda's hands. 'It was truly him?'

'No, my Lord. I haven't named anyone anyway! I was trying to say that …'

'No?' Robert roared the word, but gathered himself quickly, 'Mathilda, Eustace is gathering the family to sort this out. If you're wrong, there will be hell to pay.'

Mathilda battled to keep her own irritation in check as she responded. 'I was trying to speak, but no one was listening. Do any of you in this family ever listen to a whole sentence before you jump to conclusions and bound off to act?'

To stop Robert charging off himself, Mathilda wrapped her small fingers around his, making him look at her, puzzled endearment putting an abrupt cap on his anger.

'I have been unjust towards you, and you have heard the rumours about me, and yet you take my hands anyway?'

'As I said, my Lord, you and your brothers are used to acting hastily. Perhaps you won't in the future?' She smiled at him, knowing that there was little chance of that as she added, 'As to the latter, well, the world is built on rumours. Most of them are wrong. Why else would Our Lady denounce it as an abomination?' Mathilda stared into Robert's eyes, noticing how they were slightly mottled, more like the green of an oak leaf nearing autumn than just plain green.

Speaking with more confidence than she felt, Mathilda said, 'I think I know who Master Hugo's killer is. It is the only theory that makes sense in the circumstances, but who is going to listen to the likes of me? We need proof.'

'We won't if Eustace gets hold of him first. He'll wring his neck before any questions are asked!'

'But I think my Lord Eustace is wrong … well, partly wrong, my Lord!' Panic knotted Mathilda's stomach, 'And anyway; the man isn't worth hanging for. Will you help me? Will you help me show them the truth about Hugo?'

Robert traced a hand over the girdle at her waist, the gleam to his eyes showing some of the potential affection he'd hinted at during their first meeting. A kindness and caring that had been missing since Hugo had lied about her work at the market. 'It really isn't true, what they say about me and Master Hugo.'

'I know. I think perhaps it may have been for Master Hugo though.'

Robert bristled, but Matilda reached up and put a palm on his cheek. 'He was always going to be jealous of any friendship you had, and I doubt he ever understood why, and that made him bitter and angry.'

'You speak about things you are forbidden to even think.'

'Says the man whose family operates its own brand of law and is personally connected to many felonies. Does that make you a forbidden thought as well, or simply a member of a family with the guts to fight back against a country so corrupt that even the Queen has risen up against her King?'

Studying Mathilda, as if he was seeing her properly for the first time, Robert struggled to pull his mind back to the urgent matter at hand. He rubbed his temples. 'So do you think my brother Richard killed Hugo or not?'

'He didn't.'

'But Eustace said he'd reached the same conclusion as you, and that was …'

Mathilda reached up on her tiptoes and placed a finger

over Robert's lips, 'The rector of Teigh is in this up to his neck, but I don't think he was the one who struck out with a dagger. Nor do I think he arranged the death. Oswin and Allward will have to help us, and we have to move quickly. There isn't much time and they'll have some miles to travel.'

They moved fast. With a hasty explanation to Sarah, Robert buckled his sword to his side and made sure his dagger was still where the housekeeper had hidden it. Meanwhile Mathilda gathered up some bread and flasks of ale for Oswin and Allward, hastily stuffing them into their panniers as the boys clambered up onto the nearest horses as fast as the stable boy could saddle them.

'You know what to do?'

Oswin nodded at Mathilda as he and Allward whirled their mounts towards the gates, 'I'll see you soon, sister. Be brave.'

A lump formed in Mathilda's throat as she watched them leave, but there was no time to indulge in tears. Robert was talking to Sarah. As she hurried over to them she could hear Robert chastising the housekeeper for telling Mathilda of the rumours concerning him and Hugo. 'Of all people, I didn't want her to think I was like that!'

'And she of all people needed to know so she could be prepared for the comments.'

'And what if she believed it? What then?'

Mathilda rolled her eyes, 'We don't have time for this!' She pushed Robert towards the door as if he was a child refusing to go and fetch the firewood before a storm, 'I've already told you I don't believe it. Now go! If Eustace kills the rector, then we'll never know the whole truth for certain!'

As Robert vaulted onto his horse, Mathilda caught hold of his bridle, 'Stay safe, my Lord.'

Feeling unexpectedly warmed by the gratitude in his eyes as he held her stare for a second, Mathilda watched Robert canter from the yard, trying to catch up with Eustace and Walter before they reached Leicester, and John Folville took the law even further into his own hands than usual.

Mathilda paced the hall, kitchen and bedrooms, fussing and tidying as she went. Having given up any hope of resting after her sleepless night, she was supposed to be helping Sarah prepare the food that was bound to be desperately needed by the time the family returned. But after proving herself too distracted to be of any use in the kitchen, Sarah had sent Mathilda to attend to the fireplaces.

Her hands and knees were black from where she'd become careless in her agitated state. As the hours passed, Mathilda privately went over and over her theory, and with each pass she became less certain she was right after all. If only Allward would return and confirm her suspicions – but as she'd sent him on a lengthy trip she judged he'd be some time yet.

Mathilda began to consider what might happen if she was wrong. And even if she wasn't wrong, what would she do if Father Richard managed to persuade his brothers that she was a troublemaker bent on destroying the family?

Returning to the hall to polish the well-worn wooden surface of the hall table for the second time that hour, Mathilda began to plan her emergency escape.

~ *Chapter Twenty-one* ~

Having run through the house, peering around every door searching for Mathilda, Sarah eventually found her smoothing the covers on Robert's bed. 'Allward's back.'

The colour drained from Mathilda's face as she hurried after the housekeeper, back through the manor to find the exhausted, red faced, servant sitting at the kitchen table drinking heartily from a flagon.

'And?' Sarah demanded in her most imperial manner.

Wiping a sleeve across his mouth, Allward, breathless from his gallop, said, 'You were right.' He pointed at the evidence he'd bought with him, which was now lying on the kitchen table.

Mathilda's eyes flicked over the boy, checking him for damage, as she asked, 'And Oswin, did he get to Twyford?'

The boy nodded. 'I met him as I left Bakewell. You were right. Your father was tricked into a corner he couldn't get out of.'

'Are he and Matthew all right?'

'Oswin has them with him. They'll be safest at the Coterel manor until the guilty have been dealt with.'

Mathilda felt sick with shame. She hadn't considered the danger her accusations might have put her family in if Father Richard decided to ensure the silence of the only person who could point the finger at him with unshakeable confidence.

Placing a hand on Mathilda's arm, Sarah said, 'They'll be safe with the Coterels.'

'But they are felons.' Even as she spoke, Mathilda remembered how kind Nicholas Coterel had been to her by not taking her belt. And by sending Oswin to trail her, he had perhaps saved her life once already.

Smiling, Sarah said, 'They are as felonious as the Folvilles, but only when they have to be. Only when there is no other action left to take.' The housekeeper paused, her smile becoming set and grim, before saying, 'I fear for one of them, though –things have gone too far. The taste for the suffering of others has become a habit rather than an unpleasant, but necessary, tool to survival.'

A thunder of hooves from outside sent a tired Allward scurrying into the yard to help with the horses, followed by Sarah, her best haughty expression on her face, and an increasingly pallid and apprehensive Mathilda.

All the Folvilles were gathered in the yard.

Eustace, John, Thomas, Walter, Laurence, and Robert were moving as one. Right in the middle of them, like prey caught by a hunting pack, his face on fire with rage, stood Richard Folville, the rector of Teigh.

Bundled from the yard into the hall, the rector unleashed a feast of unholy verbal protestations as his eyes fell on Mathilda.

John, reverting to his role as head of the household, stood intimidatingly close to Mathilda, acting as if she was the one about to go on trial, rather than Richard.

'You had better be able to explain yourself extremely well, Mistress Twyford. I wish to know why you are besmirching the name of my most reverend brother. He is, you may be interested to know, the very brother who was responsible for bringing you here to pay off your errant father's debt and his unworthy defamation of Robert. For that we owe the rector for upholding the family reputation, and therefore should be showing him gratitude, not showering him with this suspicion.'

A smug expression grew over the churchman's face as he listened to his older brother cast suspicion on their hostage.

Seeing the anxiety on Mathilda's face, Sarah laid a hand on her arm before addressing the Lord of the manor herself, 'If you please, my Lord, it is the fact that my Lord Richard is responsible for bringing her here that first caused this suspicion to be cast. I beg you, for all the times you have trusted my instincts before – I truly believe you should hear what the girl has to say.'

John studied his housekeeper's face for some time. The entire room seemed to have frozen, poised for the eldest Folville's reaction.

At last, John gave a begrudging signal of agreement.

Sarah squeezed Mathilda's shoulder. 'Go on, my girl. Tell my Lord John everything, just as you told me.'

With a glance at Robert's grave countenance, which was punctuated by a flash of an encouragement in his eyes that Mathilda hoped had really been there, and wasn't a trick of her imagination, she began to speak.

'My Lords, as I tried to say earlier, there is guilt with your holy brother, but I do not believe that he wielded the dagger that slew Master Hugo, he merely wished to …'

'What?' John was ready to burst with anger, as Richard swaggered away from the dropped hold of his brothers. 'You, a hostage, had my kin hunting the entire Goscote Hundred, and across into Rutland to Teigh, for a cleric, and have them drag him here to be accused of – what, then?'

Mathilda was gratified to see that as Robert let go of the churchman, he appeared extremely uneasy about doing so, as he deferred to his eldest brother for instruction.

Burying her nerves as deep as she could, Mathilda bunched her fingers into her palms until her nails dug into her skin; the mild pain giving her an odd sort of reassurance. It seemed to be telling her that while she was still alive, she should feel every sensation possible. 'Please, my Lord, I can explain.'

'You'd better. For evil, unfounded accusations against a man of God are enough to send you straight to hell, Mathilda.'

Flinching, Mathilda stood her ground, and spoke as fast as she could. 'My Lord, Father Richard did not strike the blow that murdered Master Hugo, but he knows who did, he knows why, and I believe he has used those facts to his advantage.'

~ *Chapter Twenty-two* ~

There could be no denying that Father Richard hadn't expected the girl to say that. He'd been braced to be accused of murder, something he could easily prove he didn't do. His face darkened, and he began to protest, but not fast enough for his brothers to have missed his split second of surprised hesitation.

Ignoring his younger sibling's blustered mutterings, John's eyes narrowed, 'Go on then, girl; tell us which gullible fool you believe to have been taken in by my reverend brother enough to kill for him?'

'And more important than that,' Eustace added, keeping his eyes trained on Richard, 'hurry up and tell us why you think that happened, before I beat it out of you.'

Mathilda had been ready to blurt out a name and then run out of the hall as quickly as she could, positive that the room would erupt into a thunder of denial and threats of recrimination the second her accusation was made. In her fear however, she'd temporarily forgotten the basis of the assembled brothers' motives for crime. Yes, they were violent, but they were only violent to those deemed deserving of such treatment.

Lines from one of her favourite ballads came to her. '*Robyn loved Oure dere Lady: For dout of dydly synne, Wolde he never do compani harme. That any woman was in.'*

Robyn and his men may have terrorised the rich and avaricious, but their devotion to Our Lady meant it would go against their principles to harm a woman. Mathilda hoped that was a principle Robert and his family upheld as well. When it came to Eustace and especially the reverend, however, she rather doubted it.

'It was the dagger in my cell that made me suspicious of the rector, my Lord.'

Mathilda was about to continue, but the reverend Folville had seen his chance and pounced upon it.

'If anyone in this cursed hall would do me the justice of listening to me instead of that chit, I can tell you exactly why this child is hell bent on pointing the finger at me. She wishes to cover up her own guilt. For it was, without doubt, Mathilda herself who thrust the dagger into the chest of Master Hugo and left him to bleed to death like a suckling pig.'

'What?' Mathilda opened her mouth for further words to come, but none did, for John had sprung forward and placed a gloved hand over her mouth.

'Your manners are sadly lacking when it comes to listening to a man of the cloth, girl. You will allow us to hear him out.'

Mathilda had expected the rector to try and switch the blame to her, but she hadn't thought he'd jump in so fast. A new level of fear prickled her flesh, covering her in a cold clammy sweat. Why hadn't she started by naming the guilty party and working backwards from there? Foolish!

Striding towards John, Robert, with an expression that could have withered the crops in the fields, said, 'I would consider it a great personal favour if you would remove your hand from Mathilda's mouth, brother.'

Again, the tension in the air thickened as all eyes moved away from Richard to John and from John to Robert, as the eldest brother spoke with insincere calm, 'Can you assure me that your waif will remain quiet, and give our reverend brother time to tell his side of the story before she utters another word in accusation?'

Robert placed his hand over John's and pointedly lowered it from Mathilda's lips. 'I can, if you can assure me that, after Richard has spoken, Mathilda will be allowed to tell her side of the tale with the same courtesy extended to her?'

John paused for longer this time. 'Agreed, but she must be able to prove her words.' The elder brother paused again, before adding, 'On the surety of your place in this family?'

Sarah gasped and looked at Mathilda, the woman's eyes pleading with her to keep her lips closed, whatever lies were about to pass the churchman's lips.

Robert took over the questioning, his face etched with a menace his reverend sibling was either blissfully unaware of or was simply ignoring. 'Go on then, brother: what was Mistress Twyford's motive for murdering a man she doesn't know?'

'Isn't it obvious, dear Robert? Jealousy.'

Taking a draught of ale, Eustace sat on the nearest chair and put his feet up on the table, as if to prepare himself for the forthcoming charade, asking lazily, 'Jealous of what?'

'Master Hugo himself, naturally.' Sneering each word with relish, Father Richard then played his trump card. 'The leatherworker's ungodly affection for our dear Robert is well known. His very existence is a threat to young Mathilda, who has obviously set her sights far above her station at this family. Pointlessly, of course, as dear Robert will never take more than a token wife.'

The dagger was drawn from Robert's side in a flash of mesmerising silver before the churchman's final word had been uttered, making Sarah and Mathilda draw in sharp intakes of breath.

Although John swiftly placed a warning palm on his shoulder, Robert didn't move the blade from the rector's throat, as he hissed, 'Go on then, cleric; carry on speaking your poison while you can.'

'You place a blade at my throat! You, who bring disgrace upon this family!'

Eustace's narrowed eyes turned to John, who said, 'Lower the knife, Robert, but keep it to hand. Now, Richard, tell your tale quickly before our patience snaps.'

Holding himself as though shamefully affronted, the rector ignored all those present except for John. 'As I was saying, the girl has seen a chance to improve her family's status. The removal of her rival for Robert's affections is motive enough, and yet this girl is cleverer than that. She had a secondary plan. By implicating me in Hugo's death, she also took the opportunity to remove one of us, therefore increasing her would-be husband's share of the family wealth.

'Greed. Jealousy and greed again, John. I've seen it many times in the parish, I'm sad to say. Those believing themselves better than they are will go to any means to improve their standing.' The clergyman shook his head as he spoke, as if he was constantly let down by the folly of his fellow humans.

Mathilda's lungs felt heavy. She'd barely taken a breath as he'd spoken. Surely the brothers wouldn't believe him? It was ludicrous, especially the last bit. Although people did kill to improve their position, there was no physical way she could have got to Twyford. She had been here all the time –

locked in a cell no less!

'I myself saw the dagger by the Twyford girl's feet in the cell. Where, I should point out, she'd been thrown for repeated insolence. A dangerous game to play indeed, especially as her help and good behaviour relate directly to how soon the debt her family owes is paid off. A fine example of how poorly she regards her father and brothers.'

Robert's hand gripped his dagger handle tighter as Mathilda bit her lips so hard together that she was close to drawing blood. There was no way she was going to rise to the bait. She knew how thrilled the rector would be to see Robert thrown from the family manor.

'An interesting theory Richard. So tells us, where did she get a dagger from?' Eustace spoke as if he was relishing the show he was watching. 'You yourself ensured the girl was weapon free when she was ushered here, and you are the one who escorted her to the cell on her arrival. Are you saying you were lacking in your duties?'

Mathilda relaxed her jaw a fraction. Was she imagining it, or was Eustace enjoying this? She'd certainly got the impression earlier that he had no trouble in picturing Richard as the orchestrator of Master Hugo's death. On the other hand, the rector was his brother …

'It is hardly difficult to pick up a dagger in this house, brother! She could easily have secreted such a small weapon within the folds or sleeves of her clothing.'

'And what know you of women's clothing, Father?'

Eustace's dig caused Walter to grunt derisively, as the gloating rector barbed his reply with heavy implication, 'I suspect I know as little as dear Robert does.'

It was a snide comment too far. Robert moved so fast he was a blur. The clatter of the nearest chair hitting the floor ricocheted around the stone hall as Richard was lifted off his feet, his back slammed against the table with such force that Eustace had his flagon knocked from his hand.

'Enough! I've lived with your evil whispering long enough. No more.'

Keeping the flat of his free hand pressed against the rector's chest, pinning him against the table, Robert addressed John. 'I believe you should let Mathilda speak now, my Lord. You have heard our reverend brother. His version of events has more holes than a broken fishing net.'

~ *Chapter Twenty-three* ~

Rather than ask Mathilda to speak, John Folville turned to Sarah. 'You have been in charge of the girl while she has been here?'

'Yes, my Lord. She has been a great help to me. I admit I wasn't confident of her at first, but she has earned my respect.'

'John, you can't take the word of a servant over...'

The lord of the manor put up a hand to stem Richard's protests.

'And in your opinion, Sarah, is it even remotely possible that Mathilda could have laid her hands on a dagger and escaped from this household for long enough to kill Hugo, or even arrange for another to do the deed? Has she appeared in any blood-soaked clothes? Had a weapon in her possession? Did this dagger in the cell even exist?'

Sarah glanced at Mathilda, before confirming that there had been no time in which Mathilda could have committed such a crime. The only time she had been separated from the girl was when she was being escorted to and from Derby market and the woods by Robert, when she delivered the messages to Nicholas Coterel.

Licking her lips, Sarah nodded towards Robert as she went on, 'My Lord Robert gave Mathilda a dagger to keep on her during her first trip to see Coterel.'

'You see! She did have a weapon.'

The reverend's cry resulted in Robert shoving him even further up the table, hissing through clenched teeth, 'Sarah has not yet finished speaking. Mathilda held her tongue as you uttered your lies. Now you listen to some truth for once in your miserable life.'

Carefully Sarah continued, 'The knife was safely hidden under her cot on her return, awaiting the chance to be given back to my Lord Robert. It wasn't long after that that Mathilda was falsely accused of poor behaviour at the market when selling wares for Master Hugo and was placed back in the cell. There was no dagger on her when she went in. I put her in the cell myself. There was, however, a dagger there when I took her food and drink. The girl had fallen asleep while she was in there. During that time, the dagger was placed by her feet. I can only assume that whoever had placed it there had searched her quarters and found it.'

Lord John stared shrewdly at Richard. 'I believe you were at the manor that day, brother. Did you check on our captive, by any chance, and add something to her cell?'

'As God is my witness, I did not! The housekeeper is bound to stick up for the girl. We all know she'd do anything to protect her favourite and find a wife for her precious Robert.'

Ignoring the fresh outburst from the man pinned to the table, John refrained from mentioning that he thought God had more sense that to bear witness to his malevolent brother. 'What did you do with the dagger once you'd found it, Sarah?'

'I hid it in the kitchen and then later returned it to my Lord Robert.'

'I see.' John sounded solemn. 'I think it is time we heard

more from Mistress Twyford. However, I feel it prudent to remind you, girl, that you are not a guest here, you are a ransom. My hostage.'

John closed his eyes to collect his thoughts before adding. 'You were telling us that there was a dagger in your cell when you woke up, but not beforehand. That was what alerted you to thinking that Father Richard was involved in this matter. Yes?'

Swallowing to moisten her fear-dried throat, Mathilda replied, 'that's right, my Lord. As Sarah said, I was in the cell when Master Hugo's body was discovered and …'

'So what! You could have stuck him before then; we don't know the hour of the crime, just the hour of the body's discovery!'

The withering glare that Robert gave the rector instantly silenced the clergyman anew. Mathilda noticed that which each fresh protest of his innocence, Richard was losing his red-faced flush of angry bravado. He was beginning to go pale. That meant he was getting rattled. Perhaps he was afraid she could prove he'd committed a crime after all.

Robert smiled kindly in Mathilda's direction. 'Go on, it's all right.'

'Thank you, my Lord.' Mathilda wiped her perspiring palms down the front of her dress. 'As Sarah said, the dagger was the one that my Lord Robert had lent me, but I hadn't seen it from the moment I stowed it beneath my cot until I awoke to find it in the cell.'

'And you believe that was the dagger that killed Master Hugo?'

'No, my Lord, I think that is what everyone was meant to think. I suspect however that it is a very similar weapon to the one used. You all wear daggers, and although I haven't been here long, I have noticed that they closely resemble each other. Not only that, but if they were made locally, then many other people could also own similar weapons.'

Eustace pulled his dagger from its sheath and held it up to Mathilda, 'They were a gift. We each received one when we came of age. Most of us have other daggers we favour and keep these just for show. I rather like to keep mine handy; it has a short blade useful for hooking stones from my horse's hooves, opening stubborn locks, and such. They are more tools than weapons.'

'But they could be used to kill, my Lord.'

The single stone in the hilt of Eustace's dagger shone red in the firelight. 'Indeed they could.' He turned to Robert. 'Where is your dagger now?'

'Wrapped in an old tunic at the bottom of the chest at the foot of my bed.'

John nodded, 'Sarah, fetch Robert's dagger from its hiding place.'

As Sarah left the hall, the expectant eyes of all the men fell upon Mathilda. 'When I learnt that the leatherworker had been stabbed while I was under lock and key it was too much of a coincidence for there to be no connection. I'd only recently been introduced to Master Hugo. Shortly after that he lied about me to Lord Robert. Then, on my trip to Bakewell, I learnt that the Coterel family were suspicious of him. Then a dagger was put in my prison. And all this occurred within a very short period of time.

'It wasn't until I discovered it was Father Richard's idea to use me as a hostage to meet my father's debt that I began to wonder if he could be involved, although I didn't understand why.'

'But now you do?' The hall had become very tense. John's voice was barely above a whisper. The fire had died down and apart from the intermittent crackle as the logs snagged against the low flames, all that could be heard was the hush of suspense.

'It was after I'd spoken to my youngest brother that it all began to make sense. You see, my Lord, unbeknown to me, Oswin had overheard my father talking to the rector in the workshop a few weeks before I was bought here. Being only a woman, I was not privy to the financial arrangements my father was about to make.

'The reverend had come for some cheap candleholders for his church. We were desperate, my lord. We only had enough money needed to buy the raw materials for his pottery order, so my father took up the rector's offer of a loan and borrowed a small amount from your good selves.

'Father Richard told my father that if he would fan the flames of a rumour he had heard around the villages and towns about my Lord Robert, then he would ensure my family wouldn't have to pay back the full amount owed.'

'A rumour I suspected came from his foul tongue anyway!' Robert increased his pressure against the trapped cleric, his voice sounding incredulous as he turned back to Mathilda. 'And your father believed him?'

'Your brother is a churchman, my Lord. And my father was desperate.'

Robert growled, as he rounded on Richard, 'I assume that you, rather than keep your word, my holy brother, then reported to my Lord John that not only did the Twyford family owe us money, but that they were the people who'd begun spreading the evil rumours about my friendship with Master Hugo in the first place?'

John nodded gravely to confirm the truth of the allegation. There was no need for Mathilda to confirm Robert's statement.

The lord of the manor's steely eyes fixed themselves

upon the reverend. 'Let me guess what happened next. You came up with another plan; a plan to make it appear that you remained loyal to this family by attempting to stop the rumours that could ruin my brother and Hugo's names. By kidnapping Mathilda as a guarantee for the debt, you made it appear as though you were teaching the originator of the lies a lesson; with the added bonus of a sly suggestion in Eustace's ear that perhaps, despite being of lower status, the girl could be a suitable match for Robert.

'A move that would certainly quash the talk behind hands about his ungodly behaviour. A tattle which, I repeat, you started in the first place.

'I assume you thought Robert would be insulted by the suggestion of Mathilda's suitability for him – another fact you'd have enjoyed. How disappointing it must have been for you to see that despite the manner of her arrival here, the girl has been of considerable help to this family – and has obviously caught our brother's eye in truth.'

Raising a warning hand towards Robert, who was plainly ready to commit murder there and then, John signalled to Eustace, who rose from his chair and sauntered closer to Father Richard. Walter, Thomas and Laurence followed suit, boxing their reverend brother in against the table.

'Is there more, Mathilda?' John appeared troubled rather than angry now. 'So far you have highlighted the dubious character of my brother; which comes as no great surprise to anyone. But what you've told us seems to have nothing to do with the actual murder.'

'Exactly!' Feeling the menacing presence of his family closing in on him, Father Richard demanded, 'How am I supposed to have skewered the man while I was here, supposedly planting a weapon on the girl?'

John was losing patience. 'Mathilda did not say you

killed Master Hugo, but that you'd used the event to your advantage.'

'I did no such thing. The chit has far too much imagination.' Far from sounding relieved, the cleric looked more wary than before as he blustered, 'I've had enough of this indignity. I have souls to save.'

'Any soul in particular, brother?' Robert let go of the rector with an expression of distaste. 'Your soul perhaps? Or another soul? One that you might save all the way to the coast, so he can escape across the sea?'

'I have no idea what you mean!'

'Really? You don't know much today, do you?' said John. 'You don't wish to take this opportunity to come clean? You wish the girl to tell us more about how she saw through you?'

'John! How could you even think this of me?'

'Easily, after the number of crimes you've committed without our consent in the past.'

'As have you!' The clergyman puffed his chest in defiance.

'True, brother. But usually for the common good and never against a member of my own family!'

Mathilda thought back to the death of the corrupt Roger Belers and how much safer the region had felt after his removal, although the ripples of the terror had been felt for a long time afterwards. She thought of her suspicions that the recent meetings between the Folville and Coterel families were the build-up to the removal of another corrupt official in the near future.

John called for Allward. 'Go and fetch the sheriff, boy.'

'Are you mad?' Father Richard was shouting now. 'He hasn't even bothered sending his men to investigate Hugo's death. Not a single solider has been dispatched, nor a question been asked, and the hue and cry was stood down before it had even begun. He couldn't care less.'

'And why do you think that was, dear brother?'

Richard's mouth dropped open. 'You?'

'Master Hugo was an unpleasant and objectionable man, but Sheriff Ingram knew of his war-forged friendship with Robert, so he consulted me on the matter of his death. He agreed to leave things alone. Having a member of this family implicated in this crime would not be in the sheriff's interests at the moment.'

The rector's mouth dropped open, 'The sheriff is in your pay?'

'We have a plan afoot, do we not? We will need Ingram on our side. Anyway, he is a friend.' John answered smoothly, 'and now I think we require his presence in our home.'

~ *Chapter Twenty-four* ~

The fear now emanating from Richard was enough for John to raise his hand, to stop the already travel-weary Allward heading off on his next mission.

'Why not? Tell me, little brother.'

Richard searched the remaining family faces for a glimmer of help, but every expression was closed and sombre. Eventually he spoke with bitter resignation, 'You know full well why not. Ingram impressed upon me last time we engaged each other professionally that all my chances had run out. I don't wish to meet the hangman's noose.'

John gestured to Sarah for some ale as he sat back at the hall table with a thump. 'I imagine I can persuade him not to stretch that neck of yours, Richard, but only if you tell us the truth now. I suggest you talk.'

The reverend remained silent. To Mathilda it was as if his malevolent eyes were searing into her soul.

'No? Then perhaps we should ask Mathilda?' Pausing long enough to be sure that no response would be coming from the rector, John once again addressed Mathilda. 'So, who did kill Master Hugo?'

Summoning up all her courage, Mathilda said, 'I believe it was the potter, Geoffrey of Reresby, my Lord.'

The original incredulity returned to John's face, 'I can

see no reason on this earth why Reresby would risk his neck to kill Hugo?'

Robert lowered his dagger a fraction, reassuring himself that his brothers weren't about to let Richard flee. He moved closer to Mathilda and gestured toward her girdle belt. 'Would you be so kind as to remove your belt for me? And Allward, go and fetch the pitcher you collected from Bakewell.'

'Explain yourself, Robert.' John leant forward in his chair, his hand rubbing his short, neatly trimmed beard.

'This brings us to the matter that Coterel and Oswin suspected and led Mathilda to stitch the two sides of this tapestry together. Whatever you thought of Hugo, he was an excellent craftsman. If you inspect the belt closely, and then the borrowed pitcher, you will see that they bear exactly the same design. As you know, I was presented with the leather belt as a gift from Hugo some months ago. He was indeed gruff, uncompromising and given to being surly, but he was my friend. He saved my life when we were comrades in arms on the fields of Scotland. I owed him a debt of friendship, and I stuck by him, paying that debt.'

'A friend! You'll burn in hell! It just so happens that someone did the world a favour and sent Hugo there early!'

'ENOUGH!' Eustace was bored with the drama he'd previously been enjoying. His glare told Mathilda that there were now two brothers who would like to wring the cleric's neck there and then, so they could all get on with whatever they'd normally be doing.

Passing the belt to John, Robert took the pitcher from Allward. 'As you can see, the patterns on both items are the same, even down to the leaves and vines that wind around the diagonal lines.'

Giving everyone but the rector the chance to examine

the identical designs, Robert continued. 'When Mathilda worked at the market for Hugo she spotted Geoffrey of Reresby watching the stall. She believed that he was there keeping an eye on her. After all, he was partly responsible for the collapse of her father's pottery business, with his cheaper imports and his own decorative wares, and, always jealous of her father's greater skill with clay, had remained a thorn in the family's side for some time.'

Mathilda was grateful for the constant presence of Sarah, who kept a comforting hand on her shoulder, as John asked her, 'Did Reresby speak to you, girl?'

'No, my Lord. I did my best to keep out of his way. But I'm convinced Master Hugo saw him watching the stall; and, of course, he knew I was wearing one of his belts. I can only assume that Geoffrey did see me and noticed that my belt bore the same pattern as had so recently begun to appear on his pottery.'

'Are you telling us that Hugo was murdered because of a pattern on a pot?'

'Prior to my time working with Master Hugo I had not seen more of his work than this belt. I assumed that he had stolen the pattern from Reresby, but I was wrong. It was the other way about. Reresby had stolen the pattern. The design is Master Hugo's signature, my Lord. It seems he is known for the pattern. I have no doubt the leatherworker regarded Reresby's taking of the motif as theft.'

'Which is precisely what it was. Theft.' Robert handed the girdle back to Mathilda. 'To steal another man's work is dishonourable indeed.'

Refastening the leather around her slim waist, Mathilda said, 'I didn't notice the connection at the time, my Lords. I was too worried about my meeting with the Coterels. It was only when I heard about the pitcher's pattern from

Oswin that I finally made the link between the patterns on the leather and the pottery.'

'And how does this concern our brother?'

'Allward told me that a man had visited my father yesterday afternoon. He wasn't sure who this man was, as he'd not been there at the time. I sent Oswin to ask our father about the meeting. After some persuading, he told Oswin that the man was Geoffrey.

'Reresby was livid apparently, and not knowing that I'd been staying here, he believed my father had sent me to work with Hugo to spy on him to gather proof that he'd stolen the pattern and was going to use that information as revenge for him taking most of our trade. He had assumed my father intended to blackmail him over the pattern theft.

'My father had no idea what Reresby was talking about and apparently, their argument soon became a milder discussion, with my father having no choice but to confide that I'd been taken into service here.'

John frowned, running a palm throw his cropped hair. 'I fail to see what any of this meeting between Reresby and your father has to do with my felonious brother.'

'My Lord, in the meantime Hugo had learnt that Reresby had been using his trademark pattern. This was the reason for his poor behaviour towards me. Not jealousy, but a suspicion that it was my family who had sold the pattern to Reresby out of spite.

'It was only moments after Reresby left my father that Master Hugo was on the way to the workshop to accuse my father of profiting from the theft. I believe he and Reresby met on the road, argued, and a dagger was drawn with fatal consequences.'

'That I can confirm, brother,' Robert had the good grace to be shame-faced, 'Hugo did indeed believe that Mathilda had been avoiding being seen by Reresby because she had a guilty conscience and not because she disliked the man so much and didn't want him to know of her family's disgrace.'

Mathilda, her whole being a mass of tension, took a swig from the mug that Robert passed to her while waiting John's reaction to what had been said. John, however, wasn't the first to speak.

'You see!' Triumph oozed from the cleric, 'The brat herself says I didn't do it. I wasn't even there. And I don't know Reresby beyond his name and trade.'

Tilting his head to one side John scrutinized every line on the face of the rector of Teigh.

Each heart thudding second felt like an eternity to Mathilda as she took another sip of drink to ease the dryness of her throat.

Robert, his expression calmer than it had been all day, said, 'But you did stumble across a happenstance that you could use to your advantage, didn't you brother. A chance to blacken my name, and then to make yourself look good by appearing to clear it again! How did it go, Father Richard? Did you come across a shocked and frightened Reresby with the body of Hugo at his feet, dagger in hand, wondering what in all hell he'd done? Did you offer to dispose of his blood-stained dagger, a dagger very similar in style from those we all own, and make him indebted to you for the rest of his life, before working out how to use his condition for your own gain?

'You'd already got Mathilda's frightened father to spread a rumour about me that, if true, could see me cut off and sent to hell. What better way to capitalise on that situation and to destroy my reputation further, than by implicating the woman who you had suggested might be a companion for me, in a murder, by placing an almost identical dagger in her cell?

What a shame for you that Mathilda here has more intelligence than you have cruel cunning.'

In the quiet that followed Robert's allegations, John signalled to Allward, who disappeared out of the hall, presumably to fetch the sheriff.

'My Lord John,' Mathilda spoke, unsure if she should break the cloak of wordlessness that had fallen upon the hall, 'one point has not been addressed. Why your holy brother was near my father's workshop at that time in the first place?'

'You know why?'

'If my father had carried out the rector's wishes and spread rumours about Master Hugo and my Lord Robert, I doubt we would have sold much leather at the market that day. No one wants to buy goods from a man who goes against God in the manner implicated, and yet we sold well that day.

'I asked Oswin to enquire further of my father. It appears he didn't tell anyone what the rector instructed him to say. He had no stomach for such blether, choosing instead to pay the full amount due. It is my suspicion that the rector was on the way to my father to discover why his evil tongue was not flourishing as he'd hoped.

'However, my Lord Richard never reached my father to make his enquiries. I believe that on his way to the workshop he came across the scene of death described and saw a chance to do more damage than even rumour can do.'

John steepled his hands before him in contemplation before he spoke; 'Sheriff Ingram was telling me the other day how the Crown needs a new force of arms to send into battle with the French. He has been charged to provide a force and is at liberty to send felons alongside honest men, instead of them sending them to gaol. I believe he'll appreciate your holy ruthlessness swelling his numbers, brother.'

'No, John!' Richard's face went far whiter than Mathilda's as he protested, 'I can't go back to that life. I've not long returned, and –'

'You will go.' John pointed to Walter and Thomas. 'Take our reverend kin to the cell. He can wait for Ingram in there.'

'But it's true! Richard spluttered as his brothers escorted him toward the door, 'Hugo loved Robert wrongly!'

This time it was Mathilda that put out a restraining hand to Robert before he could plunge his knife into Richard's heart. 'Perhaps he did love Robert; but he loved him as a friend. Fiercely and loyally after their time fighting together, seeing horrors no man should see. Perhaps you didn't know that Hugo gave the girdle to Robert as a gift to pass on to the woman of his choice? I fear you understand the nature of affection and kindness between comrades, as little as you understand it between brothers.'

'And whose fault is that? Hers!' The rector of Teigh pointed at Sarah, the accusation in his voice full of a twisted bitterness. 'She made me this way!'

~ *Chapter Twenty-five* ~

Only John, Eustace, Robert, Mathilda, and Sarah remained at the manor.

The arrival of the sheriff and two of his men an hour ago hadn't been the noisy affair Mathilda had thought it would be. Ingram had come in, his dour face solemn. Curtly acknowledging all those present, the sheriff had spoken privately with John before his men were despatched to find Geoffrey of Reresby. Then the sheriff had enlisted the services of Thomas, Walter, Laurence, and Allward to escort their now mutely sour brother from the premises, destined for a holding cell and then France.

Mixing together a stickily inviting honey tonic in a small pottery bowl, Sarah passed it to Mathilda. The housekeeper was still furious. 'I can't believe he had the nerve to blame all this on me. And to use a murder to do it! Whatever happened to the church's teachings on forgiveness and understanding? I tried to treat you all equally. I tried, but …'

Eustace, who'd been berating John from across the table for not having let them despatch Father Richard to hell there and then for all the trouble he'd caused, shook his head. 'He'll blame anyone but himself, woman. The blame is not yours. Take no heed.'

Rising to his feet, Eustace drew on his riding gloves,

'I think I'll go and make certain our holy kin has reached the holding cells at Leicester. I don't trust him not to have prayer-talked his way out of trouble and made a run for it. Anyway, I want to gallop away the nasty taste left by our clerical brother from my mouth.'

'Please, my Lords,' Mathilda peered through the fringe of hair that had fallen over her face from where she'd been staring down at her drink without really seeing it, 'Why wasn't Richard bought up here by Sarah, like the rest of you? I'm sorry, Sarah, but this really does seem to be the source of the rector's rancour.'

John shrugged, 'It's what happens. The eldest takes the title and runs the home and the younger brothers join the King's forces, help run the manor, find a trade, or are sent into the church.'

Sarah was still muttering to herself as she moved around her kitchen, 'How can I help it if he has developed a taste for causing harm! I blame that church of his. It's one thing to go in an unbeliever and learn to believe, but to take every word as zealous righteousness so any evil deed you do is all right…' She dumped the jug she'd been carrying onto the table with such a thud that Mathilda feared it would crack.

'Be careful, Sarah,' Robert hadn't spoken since they'd watched the Sheriff, his unwilling guest, and his entourage disappear out of the stable yard. His expression remained grave despite the removal of the man who'd caused him so much trouble. 'That sort of talk could land you in trouble.'

'I know.' The housekeeper visibly sagged, and for the first time Mathilda could see that Sarah was probably a lot older than she appeared to be.

Exchanging a glance with Robert and as if they were in unspoken agreement, Mathilda said, 'Sit down, Sarah. Have some of this, it's already made me feel much better. Thank you.' Mathilda passed the housekeeper the remains of the honey drink.

Seeing that Robert and Mathilda so obviously understood each other without the need to speak restored the confidence of the housekeeper, and with a dip of acknowledgment to John at the head of the table, Sarah sank down. 'I've done my best. And I know I should care for Richard as much as the rest of you, but somehow he's just not ...'

John came to her rescue. 'Sarah, he's a blight on the face of this family, and I for one will be very glad when Ingram has got him safely out of the country. Let the cursed French deal with him for a while! Now,' John scrapped his chair back across the stone flags, 'I should get back to Leicester. Robert, perhaps you'd accompany me to the stables. I think it's time we made some improvements to his place, brought it up to the standards of the Leicester house. I'd appreciate your thoughts.'

Mathilda watched the men leave the kitchen. There was no mistaking the fact they were brothers, despite the decade that had divided them from birth; sandy-haired and emerald-eyed, they stood shoulder to shoulder. John was perhaps a fraction broader in the back, a little stouter around the belly, and his face had the lines of care etched into it that came with being the eldest of such a high-maintenance family, but otherwise he and Robert could have been twins as well as brothers.

Feeling the gaze of Sarah on her, Mathilda turned her attention back to the housekeeper, 'Why are you smiling at me like that?'

'I hoped he'd come to like you. I believe my hope has been realised.'

Mathilda blushed, 'It makes no difference though, does it?' Getting up from the table, she collected the spent ale mugs, 'What has happened today changes nothing. Geoffrey killed Hugo in a fit of anger. All the rector did was use events to his advantage; it was an opportunity he saw, and he seized it. The death was a happy coincidence for him, an extra way to add polish to the slander he'd already set in motion anyway to blacken Robert's reputation and get you to love him as much as the others. My family, whether they were duped or not, still have a debt to pay off.'

Observing Mathilda as she moved to the water bucket and began to fill a bowl to clean the men's drinking cups, Sarah said, 'There is one good thing that has happened because of Father Richard's vicious meddling, though.'

'What's that?'

'He brought you to us.'

A treacherous thought at the back of Mathilda's mind took the smile from her face. But what if they never let me go again?

The Folvilles may have been unusual gaolers, but whether she'd grown fond of Robert or not, which, Mathilda realised with a start, she had, the fact remained, gaolers was exactly what they were.

Mathilda had no idea why she liked Robert. He was a felon who had believed her capable of taking part in a blackmail plot. He was a robber, a kidnapper, had planned the death of Belers and had maybe even taken part in that murder ...

He was a criminal. But then so was Robyn Hode, and he was a good man ... mostly ...

Breaking the quiet that had fallen across the kitchen, Mathilda smiled at the housekeeper. 'Did you know you scared me when I came here? I'd never been made to bathe like that before. Was that really only a few days ago?'

Sarah laughed. 'Feels like an age has passed since then,

doesn't it? Sorry I was less than friendly, but I'd just been saddled with a girl who Father Richard had described to me as "the useless daughter of a malicious debtor."

'Robert had asked me to treat you like the lady of the house for a while on top of all my other jobs, when I firmly believed you to be from a family who'd spread wild chitchat about him in the first place. I was resentful. I didn't know then that the rector's snide suggestion that you be used to show the world Robert had a woman had been a plan to fan the flames of gossip.

'I suppose Robert taking his suggestion seriously, rather than just as the insult it was supposed to be, made Richard bitter enough to grab the opportunity to try and frame you for Hugo's death when Reresby so neatly handed it to him, although he must have known it was impossible.'

'Why was the suggestion an insult?' Mathilda felt herself affronted, but she wasn't sure why.

'Because you are a tradesman's daughter. To Richard, that would be a most unsuitable match.'

Mathilda knew Sarah was right, wishing she hadn't started to secretly contemplate becoming Robert's wife. She wasn't quite sure at what point that prospect had grown into an attractive one; but it had to stop. It was simply a folly that the brothers had been happy to use to their advantage.

She'd been foolish to think that Robert had become fond of her in return. She was merely someone who'd been useful to him.

'Why was I sent to Coterel? Any one of the brothers could have gone to hear that message at Bakewell.'

Sarah sighed. 'I suspect Eustace thought it would be an insult to Nicholas to send a servant. A kidnapped servant at that. It would show the Coterel family exactly how low in the Folvilles' esteem they stood.'

'But they are to work together? They're planning something big, I know they are.'

Two high points of red appeared on Sarah's face. She spoke as if she was afraid of being overheard. 'They are. But I have asked to know nothing of the plan. I suggest you curb that natural curiosity of yours in this case, Mathilda. Knowledge like that could get you killed.'

With her hands on her hips, stalling any further questions Mathilda might have, Sarah turned her thoughts to the domestic duties of the day, 'Now, I think we should keep busy or the lack of sleep from last night will floor us before the day really gets going. Will you attend to the fireplaces properly this time, please?'

Kneeling at the grate of Robert's bedroom's fireplace, Mathilda began to pull apart the fire that she'd made up the day before. As they'd never gone to bed the night before, it didn't need more than a quick sweep, but she wanted time to think, and doing something with her hands while she did so always worked best for Mathilda.

Robert had been gone a long time for someone who was just going to have a word with his brother before he rode back to Leicester. Mathilda could imagine John telling Robert that she was to be kept here as a kitchen hand until every penny of the debt was repaid; or that now she knew that something big was brewing between them and the Coterels, that they'd have to think of a way to dispose of her body …

Mathilda's stomach churned as each new idea that came to her concerning her immediate future became more unpleasant. And what of her family? Had Oswin got Matthew and her father to the Coterels in Bakewell? Were they even safe there while Reresby remained at large, or would they end up working for that family, just as she seemed to be working for this one?

She was still on her knees, sweeping up a few dots of stray ash that had fluttered from the chimney flue, when Mathilda had the feeling of being watched. Spinning around on her knees, she found herself looking directly at the lower leg of Robert de Folville, and gasped in surprise, 'My Lord, you made me jump!'

'Something that is becoming a habit with us, Mistress Twyford.' Robert's eyes danced with a flash of mischief as he held out a hand to help Mathilda to her feet; an amusement that disappeared behind his usual more serious expression once they were face to face.

'Allward has returned with news from Ingram. Reresby is in custody. He was hiding in the church of Teigh. You were right. The whole thing was an argument that got out of hand. He was expecting my brother to come with clean clothes to replace his blood-stained garments.'

Relief flooded Mathilda from the heart outwards, 'What will happen to the potter? I thoroughly dislike the man, and his theft of Master Hugo's handiwork shows what a scoundrel he can be, but I doubt he ever had murder in his mind.'

Robert reached out and stroked a finger over the top edge of the leather girdle around her waist, 'You have a kind heart, Mathilda. Your family suffered because of Reresby's greed, and yet I think you'd spare him the noose, wouldn't you?'

Not moving, Mathilda found she couldn't answer; she was too busy being torn between not moving away from the light masculine touch that ran across her waist through the woollen fabric of her dress and the knowledge that it was improper to stay so close to the man she very much feared she'd unwisely fallen in love with. Instead she said, 'I'm sorry you lost your friend, my Lord.'

A cloud crossed Robert's face, turning his eyes from their bright emerald to a dull bottle green. 'I will miss him greatly, but I'm very sorry he misled you. I am ashamed I trusted him so readily when he accused you of betrayal. In Hugo's defence, he truly believed the accusation.'

'I know, my Lord. I understand that.'

An awkward hush descended before Mathilda came to her senses and took a step away from his caressing finger. 'I'm relieved my family can safely return to their home now, so they can get back to the paying off the debt, thank you, my Lord.'

Robert was shocked. 'You don't think they still have a debt to pay, do you?'

Mathilda's forehead creased. 'They owe your family money, my Lord?'

'The amount of money involved wasn't huge. Eustace and John are not fools. They know that money isn't as important as the family's reputation. You paid off the debt by exposing the true source of the rumours. Your father will supply us with ceramics at no cost for the next year. We will do well from this arrangement.'

'But?'

'You were only taken because we believed my holy brother's claims about the source of the rumours. If we kidnapped a family member from every household that owes us a small fee, then this house would be full to the rafters with living ransoms.'

Mathilda didn't know what to do. Could she leave now?

Robert grinned down at the top of her untidy tresses of red hair. 'You are still here because I wanted to ensure that your family was safe before I released you. After all, your father didn't actually commit the crime of hearsay we were led to believe he did. No one has much choice in anything if the rector of Teigh decrees they act, and yet your father was brave enough to resist.'

'So, my family truly is safe from yours?'

'It is. And I suspect that it will now prosper with the removal of Reresby, whom I judge will get the chance to know my holy brother a great deal better while fighting at his side in France.'

'Yes, I suppose he will, my Lord.' She looked down at his hand, which had returned to the belt, feeling its warmth through the filigree patterns of butterflies. With far more effort than she would have thought possible, Mathilda said, 'I should leave. My family will need me.'

Reluctantly lowering his arm, Robert moved away. 'John instructed me to let you leave. You have done this family; especially me, a great service. Thank you, Mathilda.'

Leaning down across the foot of height that divided them, Robert kissed her lightly on the lips and then on the top of her head.

Mathilda's heart beat faster as she dared meet his eyes for a second, before gathering up her cleaning brushes in a flurry of activity, 'I, well, I should ummm … yes, I must go home; so I should really …'

'Should really what, Mathilda?' The light amusement had returned to his eyes.

'I should return this belt. Now Richard is gone, you don't have to pretend any more. Master Hugo meant it as a present for your future wife. She should have it.'

'So he did.'

Mathilda went to unhook the girdle's catch, but Robert's hands laid themselves on top of hers. 'And as such, I am rather hoping you'll agree to keep it.'

'But, but …' Mathilda wasn't certain she'd understood him for a moment, 'you're of noble birth, and I'm only a potter's daughter.'

'Mathilda,' Robert pulled her against his chest and held her close, his warmth enveloping her like a blanket, 'I'm a younger brother in a family of seven. This kingdom is in a time of chaos. Providing I have my Lord John's approval, I can choose whomever I wish to marry. And, anyway, you are never going to be, and, I suspect, never have been, *only* anything.'

THE END

Would you like to read more?

THE WINTER OUTLAW (PREVIEW)

Prologue

WINTER 1329.

Adam Calvin's vision blurred as his eyes streamed in the cold. His breath came in wheezing puffs. He needed to rest, but he daren't. Not yet.

It was only as the vague outline of a cluster of homes and workshops came into view in the distance that he realised where his legs had been taking him. Slowing his pace, but not stopping, Adam risked a glance over his shoulder. He'd expected to see dogs, horses and men chasing him, but there was nothing. No one.

Scanning the scene ahead, making sure he wasn't running into trouble as well as away from it, Adam exhaled heavily and aimed for a building he hoped was still standing.

The last time he'd visited the tiny village of Walesby, there had been an old grain store on its outskirts. Built too close to the point where the frequently flooding Rivers Maun and Meden merged, the grain store had paid the price of a poor location. Long since abandoned in favour of a superior bake house, it was a perfect temporary hiding place for a man on the run.

Adam had no breath left with which to sigh for relief

when he saw the neglected grain store. Uttering a prayer of thanks to Our Lady for the fact the building hadn't been pulled down, he lifted the worn latch. He eased his way into the damp space, which was stuffed with rotting sacks containing all manner of rubbish.

Scrabbling awkwardly over the first few rows of musty sacks, Adam made himself a man-sized gap at the back of the room. Sinking down as far as he could, hoping both the sacks and the dark would shield him long enough for his cramped limbs to rest, he did his best to ignore the putrid stench and allowed his mind to catch up on events.

Only a few hours ago everything in Adam's life had been as it should be.

He'd been fast asleep in his cot in the small private room his status as steward to Lord John de Markham gave him.

Had given him.

Adam wasn't sure what time it had been when he'd been shaken to his senses from sleep by Ulric, the kitchen boy. He suspected it hadn't been much more than an hour after he'd bedded down for the night.

Ulric, who'd frantically reported that a hue and cry had been called to capture Adam, had urged his master to move quickly. The sheriff had unexpectedly arrived and there had been a brief meeting between him, the Lord Markham and one other unknown man. An anxious Ulric had said that rumours were flying around like snowflakes in the wind.

Some of the household staff were saying Adam had stolen something, some that there had been a death; a murder.

Either way, for his own safety, Steward Calvin had to leave. Fast.

Confused, scared and angry that his good name was being questioned, without having time to find out what was going on or defend himself, Adam had grabbed his scrip.

Pulling on his boots and cloak, with Ulric's help he'd headed through the manor via the servants' walkways.

The only item Adam hadn't been able to find to take with him was his knife. Contenting himself with lifting one from Cook's precious supplies as he ran through the kitchen, he left the manor he'd called home for the past twenty years.

With a fleeting nod of gratitude to his young helper, Adam had fled into the frosty night. Only minutes later he'd heard the calls of the hue and cry; echoes of the posse's footfalls thudding against the hard, icy earth.

Now, wiping tears of exhaustion away with the back of his hand, Adam strained his ears through the winter air. All he could hear was the busy work of the mice or rats who were taking as much advantage of the building as he was.

Glad of the water pouch Ulric had stuffed in his scrip, Adam took a small draught. He didn't know how long it would have to last him. Closing his eyes, he rested his head against the sacks that boxed him in and tried to think.

Had he outstripped the hue and cry? If they were nearby, taking the chance to rest while waiting for him to run again, then Adam was sure he'd have heard something, but there were no muttered voices, no horses panting and no hounds barking at his scent.

Adam managed to get his breathing under control. He'd been part of the hue and cry on occasions himself, and he knew such groups didn't tend to chase their quarry far, or for long. Especially not on a cold winter's night, when they could be tucked up in bed before the demands of the next working day.

With growing confidence that he'd chosen his bolthole well, Adam allowed himself to relax a fraction. Few people now lived in Walesby, since the most recent of many destructive floods, and its location meant he was only a few steps from the edge of Sherwood Forest. A desperate man could easily disappear into the woodland's depths.

As the hours ticked on, Adam became convinced that the pursuit had stopped. However, he knew that by the morning the hue and cry would be replaced with soldiers if the sheriff barked the order. His bolthole wouldn't stay safe for long.

Yet that wasn't what concerned Adam the most. He wanted to know what he was supposed to have done that warranted his midnight flight. How could he even begin to go about clearing his name if he didn't know what he was accused of?

In the meantime, where was he going to go?

OUT IN APRIL 2018

Historical Notes and References

I have taken some liberties with the exact relationship of the Folville brothers – within documents from the four-teenth century, Robert is sometimes described as the fourth brother, sometimes the youngest, and Laurence de Folville is sometimes listed as a cousin rather than a brother. Never-theless, all the Folvilles, and their felonious activities, were very much real!

Roger Belers was murdered in 1326 in the field of Brokes-by, Leicestershire. The incident was recorded in the Assize Rolls – *Just1/470*. Edmund de Ashby, sheriff of Leicester-shire, was ordered to pursue and arrest Thomas and Eustace de Folville (with others) after they were indicted in the mur-der of Belers. (<u>Calendar of Patent Rolls</u>, 1324-1327, p.250)

The most scandalous co-committed crime by the combined force of the Folville and Coterel families was the kidnap and ransom of the justice Sir Richard de Willoughby in 1332. This is this felony that I allude to as the 'future crime' Mathilda becomes aware the brothers are plotting. Eustace, Robert and Thomas de Folville (and others) were all in-dicted for this kidnap and ransom in the Assize Rolls, *Just 1/141b*.

Sir Robert Ingram was sheriff of Nottinghamshire and Der-byshire on four occasions between 1322 and 1334. <u>Lists of Sheriffs for England and Wales from the earliest times to AD 1831 Preserved in the Public Record Office</u> (List and Index Society 9, New York, 1963) p.102

The steward of the Folville Manor at Ashby-Folville was

John de Sproxton. I have only named the steward Owen for the purposes of this story.

***

The ballads and political songs within this story come from the following sources (I have modernised the English of some of them).

The Outlaw's Song of Trailbaston, Dobson & Taylor, <u>Rymes of Robyn Hood: An Introduction to the English Outlaw</u> (Gloucester, 1989,)

Piers the Plowman, Langland, W., <u>The Vision of Piers the Plowman; A Complete Edition of the B-Text</u> (London, 1987), Passus XIX, line 245.

Robin Hood and the Monk, Dobson & Taylor, <u>Rymes of Robyn Hood: An Introduction to the English Outlaw</u> (Gloucester, 1989).

A Song on the Times is recorded in the '*Harley Manuscript*' No.913, folio 44. Wright, T., <u>The Political Songs of England, From the Reign of King John to that of Edward II</u> (Camden Society, First Series, Vol. 6, London, 1839)

A Geste of Robyn Hode, Dobson & Taylor, <u>Rymes of Robyn Hood: An Introduction to the English Outlaw</u> (Gloucester, 1989), p.112, stanza 456

Robin Hood and the Potter, Dobson & Taylor, <u>Rymes of Robyn Hood: An Introduction to the English Outlaw</u> (Gloucester, 1989), p.127, stanza 17

There are many excellent references to the Folvilles, Robin Hood, and the fourteenth century in general . Here a few of my personal favourites

Books

Dobson & Taylor, <u>Rymes of Robyn Hood: An Introduction to the English Outlaw</u> (Gloucester, 1989)

Holt, J., <u>Robin Hood</u> (London, 1982)

Keen, M., <u>The Outlaws of Medieval Legend</u> (London, 1987)

Knight, S., <u>Robin Hood: A Complete Study of the English Outlaw</u> (Oxford, 1994)

Leyser, H., <u>Medieval Women: A Social History of Women in England 450-1500</u>, (London 1995)

Nichols, ed., <u>History and Antiquity of Leicester</u>, Vol. 3, Part 1

Pollard, A.J., <u>Imaging Robin Hood </u>(London, 2004)

Prestwich, M., <u>The Three Edwards: War and State in England 1272-1377</u> (London, 1980)

Periodicals

Bellamy, J., '<u>The Coterel Gang: An Anatomy of a Band of Fourteenth Century Crime</u>', English Historical Review Vol. 79, (1964)

Hanawalt, B.A.,'<u>Crime and Conflict in the English Communities 1330-1348' </u>(London, 1979)

Scattergood, J., '<u>The Tale of Gamelyn: The Noble Robber as Provincial Hero</u>', ed. C Meale, Readings in Medieval English Romance (Cambridge, 1994)

Ingram Content Group UK Ltd.
Milton Keynes UK
UKHW012119210623
423738UK00001B/3

9 781999 855260